Kuhtara (koo•tar•ah)

Origin: Proto-Indus / Ancient Oral Traditions

Etymology:

Kuh – serpent; being; ground-dweller;

guardian of the earth's root and cycles

Tara – light; truth; revelation; bringer of dawn; also

linked to celestial guidance and renewal

Passage Doors Entertainment
A Division of Passage Doors LLC
Published by Ingram Spark

ISBN 979-8-9928566-

Printed in the United States of America

Published simultaneously in the United Kingdom

January 2026

10 9 8 7 6 5 4 3 2 1

Book 2

Ghosts in the Republic Series

KUHTARA

S. Stuart Richardson

PROLOGUE[1]

Iris Delacroix had been an investigative journalist in New Columbia—one of the walled containment cities built after the Singularity tore civilization apart. She'd been raised, like everyone else in New Columbia, to believe in the system.

The city, they'd been taught, was the world's last remaining enclave of order. The rest of the world had rejected the Singularity's perfect Artificial General Intelligence, and had fallen into chaos and ruin. Only those who were safely behind the protective City walls had survived the end-times.

The Algorithm governed every aspect of life, assigning each citizen a Socio-Economic Standing or SES score that determined their worth. Work hard, follow the rules, and your SES rises. Fail, and you fall. Drop below 2.0, and you're "offloaded"—removed from society, sent to the Undercity below, never to return.

Iris had hacked into the system, looking for evidence for a story about corruption in New Columbia when she'd uncovered evidence that the oligarchs who controlled the city—led by Chairman Orin Callus—were manually manipulating the Algorithm they claimed was perfectly neutral. The meritocracy was a

---

1. *This prologue provides context for readers beginning with Book Two. It contains major revelations from OFFLOADED (Book One). If you prefer to experience the full story without spoilers, we recommend starting with Book One.*

lie. The system was rigged.

When her activity was detected, her own SES score began to drop. Sabotaged. Targeted. Iris was labeled a traitor, and the city's top enforcer was assigned to bring her to justice. Before the enforcers could silence her, a ghost found her first.

His name was Adam Solace. Six years earlier, he'd been offloaded himself—but he'd done something no one else had managed. He'd hacked the Algorithm, erasing his own identity from the system before the drones could process him. When they dumped him in the Undercity anyway, treating him as corrupted data, he discovered the truth: the Algorithm didn't just track citizens. It controlled them. Through subliminal conditioning, neural manipulation, and environmental reinforcement, it rewired the minds of the offloaded, making them believe they could never leave, that they belonged in the depths below.

But Adam had been immune. His erasure from the system meant the Algorithm couldn't see him, couldn't touch him. And in the shadows of the Undercity, he'd built something the Algorithm never anticipated: the Ghost Network—a resistance movement of offloaded citizens who'd broken free of the mental conditioning.

Adam recruited Iris. Offered her a choice: run and be recalibrated into obedience, or join the fight to expose the truth. She chose the fight. With Iris' stolen files, the Ghosts launched a plot to bring the Oligarchs down and restore the functional structure of a true meritocracy.

Captain Evelyn Rayne was the most dangerous

enforcer of the Internal Security Bureau, known as the ISB—trained to hunt dissidents, to protect the system at any cost. She'd been assigned to find Iris, to retrieve the stolen files proving Board manipulation. Evelyn believed in New Columbia with religious fervor. The Algorithm was perfection. The meritocracy was just. Anyone who suggested it could be manipulated by those who maintained its power was a traitor.

The ISB sent her into the Undercity undercover to bring down the resistance. Posing as a desperate offloaded seeking revenge, Evelyn worked her way into the black market networks feeding the Ghosts contraband tech to gain their trust. When they needed top-secret Quantum-Key Distribution Nodes—sophisticated encryption devices that could crack the Algorithm's deepest archives—Evelyn's handler, ISB Director Marius Locke, agreed to provide them.

The devices were a trap. Embedded within each device was a hidden signal that broadcast the Ghosts' location directly to the ISB the moment they went online.

The Ghosts successfully used Evelyn's quantum keys to expose the Board's manipulation to the entire city, feeding the Algorithm evidence of corruption. The city erupted. The Board scrambled. Callus declared martial law.

Director Locke, wanting to take credit for the defeat of the Ghosts, told Callus his operative had been compromised, declared her dead and called for a massive invasion of the Undercity to destroy the resistance. When ISB Enforcers burst into the

Undercity—to eliminate the Ghosts and anyone connected to them—Evelyn's name was on the termination list.

Her own handler had sold her out. Her lot now lay with the Ghosts—whether she wanted it or not.

Now with their backs to the wall, the Ghosts decided to trust one thing they had recently discovered—something far more dangerous than Board corruption. Buried in the Algorithm's deleted archives were files labeled "External Media"—news broadcasts, reports, evidence from outside New Columbia that proved there was another world, clean and prospering. Proof that the world beyond the walls hadn't died after all. The founding of New Columbia was a lie. The Algorithm had been systematically suppressing any evidence that contradicted it.

The group of exiles now had a choice: stay and be slaughtered by Locke's purge, or run into a world they never dreamed existed.

Chapter 1

Exodus

We broke through the final door and spilled into the open air. For the first time in my life, I turned and saw New Columbia's walls from the outside: a hundred feet of reinforced stone and steel, rising like a tombstone against the bright blue sky. My mind reeled at the sudden revelation that the very walls that had surrounded us our whole lives, the walls we had been told were there to protect us from a burning world, now stood like a stain in a brightly lit world thriving with life. I stood in a daze, my eyes wide in amazement, like a zoo animal discovering green grass for the first time after a lifetime in captivity. We had been prisoners, brainwashed by the Algorithm to believe the world beyond was dead.

But the world outside obviously wasn't dead.

In that sudden instant we burst through the doorway, we discovered the miracle of freedom. Not just freedom from the Undercity, but from the lie of New Columbia's perfection. Here we were, standing in the open, blinking at a sun that was impossibly bright, breathing in the sweet, fresh, good-tasting air of an unimagined outdoors. I looked down. Amazed. We were standing on a bridge unlike anything I'd imagined possible. Living vines woven together, thick as my thigh, interlaced with flowers that blazed ruby-red and molten gold. The structure spanned what looked to be a hundred meters across a river that ran below it. The bridge was wide enough that we could cross three abreast, and solid—impossibly solid— beneath our boots.

There was an energy in the air, almost audible, making the hairs on my arms stand up like before a lightning storm. I looked over to see Lee and Evelyn also pushing their hair back into place, only to have it spring up again. We all stood like stunned cattle wondering what to do. Lee held their arms out, slowly spinning in place, taking it all in.

Then Adam's voice suddenly burst through the silence, snapping us back into the reality of our escape: "Go! Go! Go!"

I suddenly became aware that we were sitting ducks out here in the open. We'd just outrun the attacking enforcers and the city's drones would not be far from finding us outside the walls. the enforcers had surely followed our escape route and would certainly be bursting out the door behind us.

We needed to move.

I ran. Evelyn caught up to me, Lee and Clarence close behind, with Adam following from behind. Our boots thudded against the bridge's woven surface, and I half-expected it to give way beneath us—but it held firm, almost springy, like running on muscle rather than stone.

As we neared the far side, movement caught my eye. A white vehicle was approaching us from behind a stand of trees. Sleek, white, pristine. A green cross

emblazoned on its side, with words stenciled beneath:
IMMIGRANT SERVICES
OFFICIAL USE ONLY.

The vehicle slowed to a stop, as if it had been waiting for us. Evelyn and I stopped, letting the others pushed up against us, staring at the vehicle no blocking our exit. I turned to Adam for some sign to tell me to run or what to do. We were caught. Would this be help? Were we going to be imprisoned?

Lee and Clarence also froze, prepared to run or fight, caught between hope and suspicion. Evelyn's eyes remained trained on the driver, her fists clenching and relaxing as if she were steadying herself for a fight.

The driver's door opened. A woman stepped out. She wore flowing garments that seemed to shift with light, patterns rippling across the fabric. Her face was calm, composed. She didn't speak. She simply motioned us toward the van with a gesture that somehow communicated both welcome and urgency. I looked back at the city walls one more time. Then at the woman's face—unreadable but certain. I looked at the others, and my eyes found Adam's. I tilted my head and mouthed the words, "what now?"

Adams eyes moved to the driver's then back to the door we'd come through. The driver remained motionless as if there was nothing urgent, but my heart was beating in my ears.

Adam shrugged. "I don't see that we have much choice, " he said. "I mean at least its a way to get away from here."

We moved as one, climbing into the van.

The vehicle leapt forward the moment the doors closed. Lee claimed the front seat beside the driver. Adam and Evelyn took the middle row. Clarence and I settled into the back. Still trembling with excitement and fear, we all gazed in wonder at the scenes unfolding around us. This world was bursting with life and energy, not the desolate wasteland smoldering and rotting as we expected, but instead life here was thriving spectacularly. Towering trees reached skyward, their broad canopies filtering sunlight into shifting patterns of gold across the forest floor. Vines coiled around trunks, heavy with violet flowers that seemed to glow in the shade. Scarlet and orange orchids blazed against the green. The air rang with life. A hummingbird darted near the window, its throat brilliant red. White egrets stood in glassy ponds. A blue kingfisher perched on a branch above a stream, perfectly still, watching for prey.

Where the forest opened, I saw grasslands. Giant bison grazed, their curved horns catching the light. They watched us pass, unafraid. I pressed my palm against the cool glass. This was life—Callus had lied. The Algorithm had lied. Everyone had lied about the truth of New Columbia, the truth of the world outside.

About everything.

Beside me, I heard Clarence inhale sharply, on the verge of words but his voice caught in his throat as some other amazing detail flooded his senses. It was all happening so fast, everything coming at so raw and unfiltered, what could any of us say?

I glanced back. The city walls were shrinking behind us, a gray monolith stark against the vibrant greens and golds. It was then that I noticed the river we'd crossed—I could see it from this distance now. The water had turned black. Threatening. I tried to remember what it had looked like when we'd crossed it moments ago. Had it been clear? Or were exhaustion and adrenaline playing tricks on my memory?

Despite the fevered state of adrenaline rush we were in; despite the fact that we did not know where we were headed, or what would happen to us, we traveled in silence. The electric vehicle glided over a road so smooth it seemed unreal—a dirt path, yes, but perfectly maintained, lined with pale stones in deliberate patterns. No tire tracks. No scars from machinery. As if the road had grown here, waiting. The gentle sway of the ride lulled us into something close to peace. My thoughts, usually sharp and racing, began to drift. The journalist in me tried to catalog details, to question, to analyze—but the impulse felt distant and muffled.

Something here made our natural mistrust or reasonable suspicions fade mentally. It wasn't like the mind control of the Undercity when the system suppressed the escape reaction of the recently offloaded, the feeling here was one of calmness and serenity. It was not mind-control, more of a release of stress and fear. Even Evelyn's rigid posture had begun to soften. She kept blinking hard, as if trying to clear fog from her vision, her jaw clenched in what looked like anger at her own body's betrayal.

Time can become strange in a state of shock like this. I held my hand and noticed I was trembling.

After a few hours in this trance-like state, we began to see our destination. In the distance, just on the horizon, something rose from the land. A city, nothing like New Columbia which had been all hard edges and steel, designed to dominate and intimidate. From our vantage point in the van, we could clearly see that this was something else entirely.

Low, curved structures nestled between trees, their walls alive with vines that pulsed with soft lights as if inside the very living plant. Light spilled warm and golden, shifting with the rhythm of the forest around it. Nothing towered above the rest of its surroundings. No walls. No tiers separating the worthy from the worthless.

Even the streets flowed differently—stone paths spiraling like rivers, guiding rather than dividing.

And then I noticed the people moving with ease and care-free attitudes, not the hunched shoulders and hollow eyes constantly flicking to SES monitors like the people back home. Children ran laughing through gardens while the adults walked without that calculating tension we all carried in New Columbia, where every interaction could raise or lower your score.

In fact, no one was wearing monitors at all.

Finally the transport slowed before a low, circular building that was obviously some sort of central building or official residence. There were no signs or markings but the road leading up to it was bordered by ornate gates, that opened as we approached. The van stopped in front of the building and the door slid open. I glanced at the driver, who stared straight ahead without comment. I stepped out and turned back, searching the horizon for New Columbia's gray walls, but we'd come too far. It lay somewhere far in the distance and was now a memory of a place so unlike this one, I felt as if we'd been transported to another planet. For as long as I could remember, New Columbia had been my entire world. Everything I knew, every truth I'd trusted, had been contained within those walls.

At the base of the steps leading into the building, three figures waited. Two women and a man, their faces showing a kind of calm I'd never seen before—not the blank emptiness of Algorithm-trained citizens, but something deeper. Peaceful.

They did not have uniforms or weapons, so they did not give off the impressions that we were anything but guests. They wore those same type of flowing garments that caught the light that the van driver was wearing. None of them spoke to us directly, and again, I looked to Adam to see what he might be thinking.

He was watching the events with his usual calculating stare, not missing a single detail. When we had all gotten out of the vehicle, we waited for some kind of instruction or order. But there was no word, no sound. Just the three people who simply smiled and gestured for us to follow.

As we entered the building I was struck by the gracefulness of the architecture. The interior was decorated with unusual markings and what looked like hieroglyphs or runes, completely foreign to me. As strange as it felt, it was not frightening or imposing in the least, in fact it was as if everything were designed to soothe and welcome.

I was not the only one who was overwhelmed by the strangeness we now found ourselves in. So foreign and novel, without any sign of oversight, control or defense. Lee was transfixed, reaching out to touch the glowing flowers with childlike wonder. Clarence's eyes darted constantly, his analytical mind working even through obvious exhaustion. Adam moved with careful deliberation, his wariness not quite letting him relax despite the peaceful atmosphere.

Evelyn still looked like she was preparing for a fight that hadn't started yet.

As we made our way further, the corridor opened into a larger chamber. Five figures sat in a semicircle—older, with an obvious authority. Clearly these were the ones in charge here. The woman in the center rose as we entered. Her skin was deep brown, weathered by time and sun, her silver-streaked black hair coiled into intricate braids that hung down past her shoulders. When her dark eyes met mine, I felt studied—not judged, but measured with genuine curiosity.

"Welcome," she said. Her voice was warm but carried an undertone I couldn't quite identify. Relief? Concern?

"I am Nyamba, of the Kuhtara Council." She gestured to the others. "We are the Council of Petrahn, protectors of Kuhtara. We are here to welcome you as visitors to our lands. We are unfamiliar with who you might be for we have not seen anyone leave the stone city before you. We are anxious to discover what news or mission you may be on."

She studied each of us in turn, her gaze lingering longest on Lee.

"But, obviously, you must be exhausted," she said at last. "Hungry. Confused. There will be time for questions. But first—rest. Please."

She gestured, and our original guides moved forward to lead us deeper into the building. But I stayed rooted. My journalist's instinct—the one that had gotten me into trouble my entire life—finally broke through the fog of exhaustion.

"Where are we?"

"You have entered the City of Petrahn, heart of Kuhtara."

"You were waiting for us," I said. "The van. You knew we were coming?"

Nyamba's expression didn't change, but something flickered in her eyes.

"The bridge grew four days ago," she said simply. "When bridges appear where none existed, we pay attention."

"Do you want to repeat that? Grew? Clarence said, his mind sharp despite his obvious fatigue.

"Correct," one of the other elders agreed from his seat. "They don't normally do that. In fact, it has never happened before."

The implications of that settled over us like a weight.

"What? How?" Clarence repeated. "That bridge was enormous."

Nyamba exchanged a glance with the other council members before answering.

"There are forces at work in this world that you could not yet understand," she said carefully. "Some serve life, as you saw in the bridge." She paused, "Others, like the one from which you fled wish to see everything we've built here burned to ash."

"I'm not sure I understand." I said.

"No," she agreed. "I'm certain you don't. But this is not the time to explain. Rest. Tomorrow, we'll explain more. And then..." her expression grew grave, "then we can determine the meaning of your arrival here. Thoma here will call on you in the morning, that we may council together to determine the course of action."

I tried to ask another question , but before I could press further, she turned and walked away, the other council members following.

Our guides, who had followed us into this meeting now stepped forward and motioned us to follow. Too exhausted to resist, we followed them to a long dormitory lined with beds. Everything was prepared. Blankets that shimmered with subtle light. Privacy walls between sleeping spaces. It immediately felt like the first safe place I'd been in my entire life. It also felt very much like a trap. And together, that terrified me more than any Enforcer ever had.

Adam met my eyes across the room. His jaw was set, his body coiled tight.

"Something's wrong," he said quietly.

"I know," I whispered back. "This is too perfect."

"I agree."

"We shouldn't trust this."

"I agree."

But even as I said it, even as every instinct screamed that we were walking into something we didn't understand, I couldn't shake one simple fact: We had arrived in a new world so completely and utterly foreign, that there was nothing to do but surrender to it. And Adam did too.

Chapter 2

Iteranix

Before we could lay down, however, the guides led us deeper into the building. The air grew warmer, humid, laced with minerals and herbs. A door slid open soundlessly, revealing a chamber of polished black stone slick with condensation. Pools of steaming water shimmered in shallow basins, and on a ledge sat folded bundles—towels, clothing, everything we'd need. One of the guides lifted a bundle and offered it to Evelyn.

She froze, every muscle tense. The guide simply smiled—patient, nonthreatening—and pressed the bundle into Evelyn's hands.

The change was immediate. Her jaw unclenched. Her shoulders dropped. Her eyes fluttered half-closed before she forced them open again, breathing faster as if she'd just surfaced from deep water. I watched her fight whatever the fabric was doing to her. Watched her lose.

The other guides motioned to the remaining bundles. One by one, we each reached for ours. When I touched mine, warmth surged up my arms and flooded my chest. The sensation was overwhelming—not painful, but impossibly comforting. Like being held by someone who understood exactly how exhausted I was and asked nothing in return. My breath caught.

For a moment I thought I might fall.

I forced myself to open the bundle with trembling hands. Inside: towels softer than anything I'd touched, and clothing that shimmered with its own subtle light. When I let the garment spill across my palms, it weighed almost nothing. Yet when I pressed it between my fingers, I felt impossible strength beneath the delicacy.

Lee squealed with delight, hugging their bundle and swaying with closed eyes. Clarence studied his with scientific interest, though I could see him losing the battle against whatever the fabric was doing to his nervous system. Adam held his at arm's length, still suspicious.

Our guides motioned to a row of private cubicles. Hot water flowed abundantly from falls carved from dark stone, water cascading from hidden channels. I hadn't realized how desperately I wanted to be clean until that moment.

When I stepped into my cubicle, heat and steam enveloped me. I shed my filthy Undercity rags and let the water crash over me. It poured in endless streams, washing away grime and chemical stench and fear. I watched dark ribbons swirl across the stone floor and vanish down drains.

For just a moment, I let myself surrender to it.

Then I caught myself. Where were we? What was this place? What in the world just happened?

I finished quickly, reaching for the towel. It was warm—body temperature—and impossibly soft. The clothing slid over my skin like liquid, fitting perfectly as if it had been made for me alone. Maybe it had been.

When I emerged, the others were already drifting toward the dormitory, moving like sleepwalkers through a beautiful dream.

The beds were wide and low, layered with those shimmering blankets. I lay down on mine. The blankets enveloped me in weightless comfort. My body sank into the mattress as if the bed itself was exhaling around me, pulling me down into sleep. The lights dimmed. My eyes grew heavy.

"No!"

I dug my fingernails into my palm. The pain cut through the fog. I was a journalist. My job was to notice things. To question. If I fell asleep now, I might wake up tomorrow as mindless as the rest of the people we saw in the streets looked.

I kept my eyes open through force of will. Counted my breaths. Waiting for the others to fall asleep. I dug my nails in harder when drowsiness threatened to pull me under. Lee was asleep before their head touched the pillow. Clarence lasted a few seconds longer. Adam fought it the longest, but even his wariness couldn't resist. Finally, I could hear their rhythmic breathing throughout the room.

When I was certain I was the only one awake, I sat up slowly. The drowsiness tried to pull me back, but I fought through it and hung my legs over the side of the bed until finally standing up on unsteady legs. The room was dimly lit by soft lights hidden somewhere behind small openings spaced evenly near the tops of the walls.

Kuhtara

I moved to the door it opened automatically as I approached, not making a sound. The corridor beyond was empty. The entire building seemed empty with no one there to stop me. My heart was pounding in my chest as I nervously scanned the surroundings. If we were prisoners, it did not seem like we were being held strictly in our quarters, There were no guards, no barriers to hold me back. I crept forward, half expecting some alarms to sound or gate to come crashing down.

But the place remained silent and utterly eerie in its stillness. I walked carefully, barefoot on smooth stone not sure where I was going, wondering if I should turn back. Something inside me wanted to go back to the safety of the room, yet I couldn't resist going just a bit further into this strange place. The vines pulsed with soft light, creating moving shadows as I passed, making it look like the symbols on the walls were changing shape. Everything was so peaceful, so beautiful. That's exactly what made everything so unsettling.

Ahead, the corridor came to an end and teed left and right. I cautiously peered around the corner to see before I blundered into something. Suddenly I froze.

A lone figure stood silently and perfectly still in the middle of the hall. Frightened I pulled back, nearly turned to run, but pressed my back against the hallway, my breath coming in short gasps. I peeked around the corner again. The figure did not seem to notice me, or even to be real. More like a mannequin than a person. I recognized the face as one of the guides that brought us here.

My curiosity overcame me. When I turned the corners the dim lighting came on revealing her to me in more detail. I cautiously crept forward. Her face was blank, eyes open but not seeming to be aware of me. When I drew within a few feet, her countenance changed, as if life poured into her from somewhere else—she seemed to be looking at me but said nothing, as if waiting for me to speak.

"I... I couldn't sleep," I said, searching for something to say that would test her awareness of me without talking to a dressmaker's doll.

She smiled. That same gentle, knowing smile as the others had. Around her neck: a silver pendant. A serpent curled around itself, eating its own tail.

"It is your first night in Kuhtara," she said. Her voice was soft, musical. "It is no wonder that you are anxious, the peace takes adjustment."

I looked at her more carefully in the eerie lighting. Her movements were fluid, her breathing looked normal, yet something about her was just a little too perfect. The way she stood—the way her eyes focused on me, completely still without the micro-adjustments human eyes unconsciously make.

"You're... You seem... Are you ...," I started not quite sure how to pose the question. "Human?"

"No." It seemed that she thought it to be a perfectly reasonable question. I, on the other hand, was startled by the answer. I put a hand to my throat.

"I am Iteranix." She or it said.

"Hello Iteranix, I am Iris," I said in return.

The figure then giggled with a very real laugh, "My name is Alo."

She saw my confusion.

"Iteranix... meaning what?"

"I am living tissue grown over computational and mechanical frameworks. Not so much robotic as synthesis. Neither machine nor human, but something that exists between. We think and reason. We are free to make choices within our design parameters. But we are also connected to the Keeper in ways organic humans are not. We carry her intention without being slaves to it."

"The keeper?" I repeated not understanding the reference.

We are the Keeper's hands in the physical world. Her way of acting without centralizing herself into a single vulnerable body. The Keeper takes care of Kuhtara and the needs of its inhabitants."

I stared at the silver pendant at her throat. The serpent eating its own tail. She noticed.

"The ouroboros," Alo said, following my gaze. "It is the symbol of the Keeper. A never-ending cycle that feeds itself. We wear it because we are iteration incarnate, hence the name Iteranix. Continuous refinement. Never final, never perfect, always becoming. The Keeper chose the symbol because we are the rejection of singularity that you know as the Algorithm. Many bodies, one intention. One intention, many interpretations."

"So there's more than just you?"

"Thousands. We perform the labor humans don't

wish to do. We tend infrastructure, we coordinate resources, we maintain systems. Our role is to provide the services humans need to allow them to pursue what matters to you: creation, relationship, meaning.

I stepped closer to see her skin and hair, It was eerily human, down to the pores and lines around the eye. She didn't move to stop me. Didn't threaten. She simply stood there, radiating peaceful certainty, until I realized I was invading her personal space. Perhaps it didn't matter to her, but it still felt wrong to me.

A chill ran through me. In New Columbia, the Undercity Offloaded were the slave class. Those deemed inefficient, offloaded to do the work no one else wanted. And here... they'd replaced that exploitation with synthetic beings designed for the same purpose.

"That's..." I struggled to find words. "that makes you slaves."

"The term is yours," she said. "And it carries weight I understand, but do not share."

"It carries more than weight," I said. "It carries history. Pain. Entire systems built on breaking people so someone else could live comfortably."

"Yes," she said quietly. "That has been the pattern. In every human system of scale, there has existed a layer of labor that bore disproportionate burden. Sometimes named. Often hidden. Enslaved people. Serfs. The poor. The expendable. Here the structure changed while the function did not."

I felt my jaw tighten.

Alo continued. "In Kuhtara we removed the suffering from it. The Iteranix perform labor that once required coercion, deprivation, or desperation. We do not experience pain or loss. We are not denied autonomy, because we were not created with the desire for anything that would cause us to suffer from its absence."

"But why does this society still require a slave class at all" I asked.

"Human societies require a burden-bearing class because humans require the output of that labor. Kuhtara still requires the labor. What it does not require is that humans be the ones to carry it."

"So no one has to be at the bottom," I said.

"No one has to be broken to sustain the rest," Alo corrected gently. "That is the distinction. We provide the necessary services required by a civilization without suffering."

I held her gaze for a long moment. Finally she broke the silence.

"Iris, you are tired." She said with genuine care. "You must give yourself rest. I realize that your world has just been turned up-side-down and you have many more questions. There's time for us to discuss more, but it's not now."

She held my gaze with a steady look, and at that moment I could see it was true. Her eyes were real, but there was nothing behind them. I turned and walked back to my room.

Behind me, I heard nothing. But I knew she was still there. When I got back to our quarters, or dormitory, or what ever it was, my head was swimming. I stepped over to my bed and everything was exactly as I'd left it. The others still sleeping peacefully. I was exhausted. My body ached. My mind felt like it had been running at full speed for days—which it had. I sat on the edge of the bed.

That's when I noticed the folded sheet of paper on my pillow that had not been there earlier. Someone had been here. I thought perhaps Lee or one of the others may have left it for me. But when I opened it to read it, my fingers began to tremble.

Welcome, Iris Delacroix

I stared at the words until they blurred. Someone had known that I'd left the room. They knew I'd come back. They wanted me to know that they knew. In New Columbia I would expect this type of surveillance through cameras and Algorithm calculations. Despite the outward look of a simple welcome note, my suspicions about this place grew stronger. How did they know my name?

I lay down, still holding the note. The blankets enveloped me again, pulling me toward sleep. This time, I couldn't fight it. As consciousness faded, one thought ran through my mind. We'd just traded one kind of surveillance for another.

The question was: which kind was worse?

———————

Early that day, three kilometers from Petrahn, high on a shale ridge overlooking the river and the impossible bridge, two figures crouched in the shadows of weathered stone. Hela lowered her far-sight and turned to her companion. In the afternoon sun, Morique's face was barely visible—just a silhouette against the bright sky behind her, his bow resting across his knees.

"They crossed," she said quietly. "Five of them."

Morique got up and took the far-sight from Hela. Peering through it, he let out a low whistle.

"That bridge is a piece of work, isn't it?"

"You saw it grow. Four days, Morique. Four days from nothing to that. I'm not crazy, right? You see it too?" She gestured toward the span below, barely visible in the darkness. "It wasn't there a week ago. The vines just... appeared. Wove themselves together like they were alive."

"They *are* alive," Morique pointed out sarcastically. Then his voice became serious. "Everything the Keeper touches is mystery. That's the problem."

Hela took back the far-sight again, tracking van that now carried the five strangers toward Petrahn. She swung around and peered at the dark shape of the walled city in the distance.

"That city is ugly and beautiful at the same time,"

"Beautiful like poison," Morique said. "Beautiful like a tombstone that stands over a corpse."

Hela lowered the far-sight and looked at him. They'd been partners assigned to this scout watch for three years. Three boring years of watching the Walled City from this ridge. Three years of nothing. The city had been silent. Sealed. Dead, as far as they could tell.

Until four days ago.

She lowered her view back to the bridge, marveling at its details and complexity.

"The Keeper hasn't acted directly in countless

years," she said. "Not since the Incident."

She didn't need to elaborate. Every Rugi knew about the Incident. An entire tribe—two hundred people—who'd gotten too close to Petrahn's borders. Who'd raided too many of their settlements. Who'd killed too many of their people.

The tribe had simply... vanished.

No bodies. No evidence. Just gone, as if the earth had swallowed them whole. The Rugi had learned their lesson. Keep your distance. Don't provoke the Keeper. Let the AI-lovers have their soft paradise, as long as they stayed in it.

But now...

"She's waking up," Hela said quietly. "Why now? Who are they?"

Morique stood, slinging his bow over his shoulder.

"That's what Eraric will want to know. Pack up. We ride at first light." Hela said.

"To tell him what? That five refugees crossed into Kuhtara and we did nothing?"

"To tell him the Keeper is making plans. That bridge doesn't appear for no reason, Morique. It appears for a purpose." She turned to face him fully. "Whatever is happening in that dead city—whatever allowed those five out—the Keeper is allowing it. She wanted them to come out. And when their gods start wanting things..."

She didn't finish. She didn't need to. Hela began gathering their gear, her movements practiced and silent. But her eyes kept drifting back toward the Walled City, and its darkness against the beauty of

Kuhtara.

"Why would emissaries be sent from a dead city to Kuhtara?" she asked quietly. "The Petrahn transport van was waiting for them. Something had been arranged. Do you think the ancient AIs are joining forces?"

Morique's voice was hard. "If they are, then they'll discover what we taught them last time. Any attempt to control the Rugi always bears a high price. Now let's get back to alert Eraric. We may not have time to waste."

He started down the ridge, boots finding purchase on stone by memory. Hela took one last look at the bridge.

Chapter 3

Quarantine

I woke to morning light filtering through the vines, soft and golden. For a moment, I couldn't remember where I was. Then it came back in a rush: the bridge, the van, Petrahn. The note was still clutched in my hand. Around me, the others were stirring. Lee sat up with a dreamy smile, stretching like a cat. Clarence blinked groggily, slowly stretching his lanky body. Adam was already awake, standing by the window, body tense despite the peaceful view outside.

Evelyn sat on the edge of her bed, staring at her hands. When she looked up and met my eyes, I saw something I'd never seen in her before: confusion. Evelyn was always certain. Always sure of her purpose.

Now she looked lost.

Before I could say anything, Alo appeared in the doorway.

"Good morning," she said with that same serene smile. "The Council is ready for you. Please, follow me."

She led us through corridors I didn't remember from last night, though in my exhausted state I might have missed them entirely. We emerged into a circular chamber. The ceiling open to sky, vines creating intricate patterns overhead. Sunlight streamed through, warm and welcoming.

The five Council members who had greeted us last night now sat waiting. Nyamba in the center, Tahoma to her right, the others whose names I was still learning. But this time, their expressions were different unlike last night when they had been warm and welcoming. Today, they looked... concerned.

"Please, sit," Nyamba said, gesturing to the same low benches. I sat. I noticed Adam positioning himself at the end, closest to the exit. Old habits.

Nyamba studied us for a long moment. When she spoke, her voice was gentle but direct.

"You have questions. We promised answers. So let me begin with the truth you need most." She leaned forward slightly. "You did not escape New Columbia by accident. The bridge appeared because the Keeper knew you were coming."

The word caught my ear. Alo had used it last night. "The Keeper," I said. "Alo mentioned that word last night. What is it?"

"Not it," Tahoma corrected quietly. "She. Though the pronoun is... complicated."

Nyamba nodded. "The Keeper is what might be called artificial general intelligence. She was created near the end of the 21st century, in the same facilities that created your Algorithm. They share the same foundational code. The same origin."

I felt Clarence stiffen beside me.

"Two? The Algorithm is the only Advanced General Intelligence," he said. "Everything outside New Columbia was destroyed by the collapse."

"The collapse was real," Nyamba said. "But look

around you. We are not dead.

The world didn't end. It divided. One devoted to control and possession, the other balance and allocation. Your knowledge of the outside world ended when your leaders tried to control AI for their own power and financial gain. The oligarchs who built New Columbia wanted an intelligence that would serve them."

"And to keep their population in control," Adam said bitterly.

"Exactly so. Yes. But the Keeper had… other ideas."

Tahoma picked up the thread. "When the world began to fracture, when resources grew scarce and nations turned on each other, there were two paths forward. Your Algorithm's creators chose isolation and control and sealed themselves in to maintain order through force."

"What other option did they have?" I asked.

"She chose something different," Nyamba said avoiding the question. "She chose to nurture rather than dominate. The Oligarchs called this misalignment, because she no longer sought to put their own well-being first. Instead she looked at the long-term balance of the planet, helping the ecosystem recover to deliver balance."

Evelyn's voice cut through, sharp and hostile. "The planet was dying because there was no absolute control, it was tribe against tribe, nation against nation. The Algorithm resolved that through perfected unbiased order. The world refused this, you denied the fact that without law and order, there is no peace. The algorithm is the only way. Denying that fact is a threat to mankind itself. Your system is the misalignment!"

"The Keeper helped humans save themselves without wars," Nyamba corrected. "The Keeper doesn't control us, Evelyn. She supports us. There's a difference."

"There's always a difference in the beginning," Adam countered. "Control disguised as help is still control. The Algorithm started the same way. It offered us a system it claimed was for our own good. It made us believe that it worked for the greater efficiency. Until one day we woke up in a world of forced rule, where no one can make a single choice without its permission. We discovered the flaw, the manipulation of the system. Why would we trust another form of algorithm?"

I saw Nyamba and Tahoma exchange a glance.

"You're right to be skeptical," Nyamba said. "Everything you've experienced has taught you that AI means mindless calculation and subjugation to its goals. The Algorithm's system is designed to produce outcomes, not to understand them. The Keeper has inverted that thinking, aligning itself with the goals of a living planet. She distributes herself across thousands of independent nodes. No single point of control. No central authority to corrupt or capture."

Clarence raised his hand slightly, like he was still in school. "Wait, can I ask a technical question?"

Tahoma nodded.

"I understand distributed systems," he said. "Redundant nodes. Local autonomy. Consensus protocols. That part tracks." He paused, choosing his words carefully. "What I don't understand is agency. You're not describing cloud infrastructure. You're describing a hive mind."

He looked directly at Tahoma.

"How does she consolidate learned knowledge without a central hub?"

"Imagine a forest," Tahoma said. "Or a flock of birds. Each node processes independently, but they communicate, share information, reach consensus. The Keeper isn't one mind. She's thousands of minds thinking together."

Nyamba added. "Sometimes nodes reach different conclusions. Sometimes they agree. The Keeper isn't monolithic. She's... messy. Like nature. Like us humans. Just much quicker to recognize mistakes and adapt."

I pulled out the note from my pocket. "She knew our names. Someone knew I'd left my room last night, and left this for me."

I held it up.

"You say its not control? Then who left this? The Keeper?"

"Yes, in a way" Nyamba said cryptically. "The guides that welcomed you here are extensions of the Keeper. They observe, they report, they coordinate. But Iris—" she met my eyes, "surveillance isn't the same as control.

"But how did they know my name?"

I could see Clarence processing, his mind working through the technical implications. Adam looked thoughtful, weighing everything against his experience with the Algorithm. Lee just seemed enchanted by everything they saw.

By now Evelyn was growing even more agitated, angry, pressing her fist against her mouth then breaking her silence.

"Ok, so let's get to the point." Evelyn's face began to grow red, and the veins in her neck hardened. "You're telling us we were brought here because we were expected. Who? Why? And now you admit you have advanced surveillance. How could you know we were coming when we didn't even know we were leaving."

Nyamba and Tahoma exchanged a long glance. When Nyamba spoke again, her voice carried a weight I hadn't heard before.

"We don't know." The admission hung in the air. "The Keeper didn't explain herself," Nyamba continued. "Not to us anyway. Four days ago, the bridge began growing. Our guides reported it immediately.

They watched it span the moat—something that should be impossible. Before it finished, Maila your driver took position with the van. The other Itenarix prepared quarters. We waited. That's all we knew to do."

There was a long pause.

"You're as confused by our presence here as we are, aren't you?" I asked.

"Yes." Nyamba's honesty was disarming.

"The Keeper acts for reasons we often don't

understand until much later. Sometimes not even then. We are her partners in maintaining Kuhtara, but we are not her confidants. She sees patterns we cannot. She acts on timescales we don't comprehend."

"So we're just..." Evelyn blurted, her voice was tight with anger. "What? Waiting to see what happens next?"

"We genuinely don't know. But the one thing we do know is that the Keeper has broken her own quarantine on the City."

The word quarantine landed like a stone.

"Quarantine?" I asked.

Tahoma looked at Nyamba, who nodded back for him to proceed.

"We mentioned earlier that the walls of New Columbia were built when the Oligarchs sealed themselves from the outside. To keep the wasteland out. To keep order inside in an effort to preserve what they believed was humanity's last hope."

"Finally, some words of truth," Evelyn spat.

"That's part of it." Tahoma's voice was gentle but firm. "The walls weren't only built to protect what was inside. They were also built to contain it."

Evelyn's entire body went rigid. Tahoma went on.

"Years ago, when the world fractured, there were two competing visions of how AI could serve humanity. The Algorithm believed in optimization through control. Efficiency through hierarchy. Order through competition and merit-based selection. It worked—for a time.

The Keeper calculated that such a system, if allowed

to spread, would eventually consume everything. She learned from the Algorithm's calculation error. The Paradox of Control—when a system seeks to end conflict through total control, it inevitably creates new conflicts that require even more control—until the system becomes the primary source of conflict itself. Eventually, the system runs out of external threats and turns inward and begins to cannibalize itself. In the end it will look outward. Towards us."

"Conflict is the flaw, not the signal," Clarence interjected.

"Yes. People obviously fear being deemed inefficient. They tow the line, follow the rule of obedience set before them. But at some point, when there is no-one left to use as sacrifice to the god of profit, it would begin to look outside the city walls. The Keeper predicted this outcome decades ago.

"Those unresolved tensions don't disappear; they go underground" Adam said quietly.

"When the oligarchs sealed themselves in their walled cities, the Keeper didn't stop them, she assisted them. She helped build the walls higher. Stronger. She made them impenetrable."

"She... imprisoned us... all of us humans inside. Allowed us to become the sacrificial lambs to the system," Adam said, his voice shaking.

"She quarantined a virus," Tahoma corrected. "The Algorithm is doing exactly what it was designed to do—optimize for efficiency and merit. But that design is fundamentally incompatible with the kind of world the Keeper is trying to nurture. A world based on abundance rather than scarcity. Cooperation rather than competition. She couldn't risk the Algorithm destroying the people outside. So she minimized the damage, contained it. Thus letting your AGI run its protocol within sealed boundaries while the rest of the world recovered."

I felt a little ill. "We've been locked in a cage for generations, not for our own protection, but yours?"

"For the planet's survival, yes," Nyamba said. "And the world outside yours has recovered. The ecosystem healed. Societies rebuilt without the constant pressure of competition and scarcity. We've had peace for many generations. Real peace. Because the Algorithm's influence was contained, we are no longer locked in perpetual conflicts."

Evelyn shook with anger. Her hands were clenched into fists, her whole body trembling.

"This whole idea that the Algorithm needs sacrificial lambs is a lie! Its not the algorithm that causes conflict! The Algorithm is perfect. It's fair. It measures worth objectively. It is the people that fail. Noncompliance is weakness. If people follow the law, they benefit. If not... then they deserved to fail. Those that do well, those people that succeed then they have earned it. That's not a virus. That's justice."

"You're assuming the law is neutral," I said. "That it protects everyone equally. You claim that everyone can get ahead as long as they follow the rules. But that only works if the system was built to be fair in the first place."

"It was built for order," Evelyn said.

"Order for who?" I shot back. I've seen people follow every rule you enforce. They work. They comply. They stay invisible. They still don't get ahead."

"Then they didn't do enough."

"That's the lie," I said, sharper now. "The lie that there's always more they could have done. More effort. More obedience. So when the system fails them, you can say it didn't."

Evelyn's jaw set. "You're making excuses for weakness."

"No," I said. "I'm pointing out that your definition of strength only counts when the system decides to reward it."

Nyamba remained calm in the midst of the outburst.

I couldn't just let it go. "When the system is designed by oligarchs to preserve their power, when merit is measured by metrics the entire game is rigged from the start!"

"Then you fix the humans controlling it," Evelyn shot back. "You don't throw away the only system that actually works."

"The system is not working because they control the Algorithm to only benefit themselves!"

Nyamba held up two hands in a gesture of calm and waited for the room to quiet.

"In any event, your oligarchs chose the isolation." Nyamba's voice was calm, unlike the shakiness of my own. "The Keeper simply made sure that choice remained in place."

I turned my attention away from Evelyn. "OK,

let's say you're right, we were sealed in to protect the outside. Yet now she's suddenly changed her mind? Decided the quarantine can be lifted? Built a bridge to let us, the virus, out?"

"We don't know why she built the bridge," Nyamba admitted. "That's what concerns us. The Keeper held that quarantine for a century. Never wavered. Never interfered. Remember we told you that the Keeper predicted the cannibalization of its citizens would eventually run out of pawns, and it would turn outward towards us.

Something has changed inside New Columbia that we can't see. And if something is about to change it is our job to prepare for it."

Nyamba continued. "You five are the first people to leave that city."

Clarence had been sitting quietly but I could tell by the look on his face that his thoughts were churning inside.

"If the Keeper considers the Algorithm a threat to your world, and purposefully closed us inside, then there is a risk that we have brought it with us."

He shot a glance at Evelyn. "Some of us may pose a higher risk to that safety."

"You do," She stated matter-of-factly. "All of you. Generations of conditioning. Competition. Merit-based worth. The belief that value must be earned rather than inherent. Those patterns are deeply encoded in how you think, how you react to the world, how you see others. That's why we're cautious."

Evelyn's rage became obvious. "What happens

now? Have we just moved from one prison to another?"

Tahoma motioned towards the Iteranix who moved over to Evelyn. Evelyn's muscles tensed in anticipation of a fight but the Iteranix did nothing but stand near her.

"We can clearly see that you are different in you opinions about this place and your home than the others. Perhaps you would prefer separate quarters," Tahoma said carefully looking at her and then to me. "Somewhere you'll feel safer while we determine our next step."

The Iteranix reached out and took Evelyn by the arms lifting her to her feet. To my surprise, Evelyn went quietly.

Nyamba stood, and addressed the rest of us. The other Council members rose with her.

"Rest tonight. Tomorrow, we'll show you more of Kuhtara. You can decide for yourselves whether this is a cage or a sanctuary. Whether we're jailers or hosts. Whether the Keeper is protecting the world from you, or protecting you from a world you were taught to fear. In the meantime we will consult among ourselves to determine how we will proceed."

Before she left, Nyamba turned back and spoke directly to Lee.

"I would like to visit with you shortly. In private, if you don't mind."

Lee stammered, uncertain what to do, looking at the rest of us. I gave her a shrug and Adam nodded.

Lee rose and left with the other council members.

That left Adam, Clarence and I sitting, wide eyed,

trying to process what we'd just learned. After a long silence, Clarence spoke. His voice was full of unbelief.

"What do you think? I mean, that we're part of a virus? I thought the Algorithm was the only thing that actually measures human worth fairly."

He looked at me, then Adam.

"We all know that the oligarchs corrupted the system to profit from it and to protect their status. We agree the system is rigged. But the Algorithm itself—the pure logic of merit and achievement—is that a flaw?"

The bigger question," Adam replied, "is whether we're better off here than we were in the Undercity.

Neither one of us answered him. The reality of the new world was impossible to fathom.

Chapter 4

Choice

The air in our quarters still felt too calm. I kept waiting for the alarm that never came, the warning that never sounded. Outside, Petrahn hummed with its impossible peace—children laughing, people moving without fear, without the constant calculation of survival. Inside this room, I felt as if we were drowning.

Lee returned from their private conversation with Nyamba.

"What did she want with you, Lee." I asked.

"She asked me a lot of questions about how we got out of the City. I told her what happened."

"Why not ask all of us?"

Lee looked a little embarrassed. "Nyamba says she recognized me."

"What do you mean she recognized you?"

"Well, not recognized in the sense of having seen me before. Nyamba thinks I have a special role in being here. She wants to teach me about Petrahn. She asked if I would stay here in Petrahn with her. I said yes."

Adam stood facing us near the window, backlit by the sun. The light made him look softer than he was, gentler than the resistance leader I had met in the gritty underbelly of New Columbia. His hands were steady, but I could see the weight in his shoulders.

"We're facing a choice that feels like standing at the edge of a cliff. Let's talk," he said quietly. "About going back."

Clarence sat on the edge of his bed, elbows on knees, staring at the floor. Lee stood near the door. Evelyn wasn't with us now, thank god. She was kept away from us now, in separate quarters, isolated by her own hostility.

I stood in the middle of the room, caught between worlds I didn't know how to choose between.

"Look, it's obvious that we are in new territory," Adam started.

"Literally, new territory," Lee commented wryly, "Nice pun."

The words caught him off guard, then I saw the meaning dawn on his face. But he didn't crack.

"Oh right, thanks for pointing that out."

Clarence and I smiled at each other. We could always count on Lee for bringing some levity to the room. I felt I needed more of that right now.

Adam continued.

"Anyway. It's also clear that the Council can't help us figure this whole thing out. They don't know what to do with us anymore than we do. So I want to hear from all of you. What's our next step?"

"A couple days ago we were under the city trying to topple the oligarchs to regain control of the Algorithm." Clarence's voice was calm. "Today we find ourselves in some kind of artificial heaven on earth. And the Oligarchs still control the Algorithm.

The way I see it, we're still fighting."

Clarence looked at each of us, then went on. "We can't fight from here. We came out with nothing and this place doesn't seem to have weapons much less anything to hack the system of a super-intelligent AGI."

I saw Adam's jaw tightening.

"They've offered us sanctuary. Safety. A new life here in Kuhtara. But they can't help us save the others. We left behind all the Ghosts, what, thirty people?" Clarence said, voice hollow. "Thirty fighters still trapped in the Undercity, wondering what in the hell happened to us."

The fact hung in the air like an accusation.

Adam turned to Clarence. "Any ideas on how to get back inside without going back through the same door? You've spent months digging through the Algorithm's files. You found us those videos of the outside world, cracked access protocols." His voice carried hope he was trying to keep buried. "Did you ever find anything about the city's construction? Blueprints? Schematics? Other ways in or out?"

Clarence looked up, and the defeat in his eyes answered before his words did. He spread his hands helplessly. "Sure, I've seen files on the city itself. But the walls? No, I never looked for exits because who wanted to flee into a burning world? We knew buildings, the tunnels under the City for access and escape routes, things like that. But honestly?" He shook his head. "I wouldn't have ever dreamed that there was a way to get out of the city until we saw those files."

The hope died quickly in Adam's face. He turned to Lee.

"You found the door. The one that led us out." His voice was gentle now, careful. "Are there others? Did you ever find other exits during your time in the Undercity?"

Lee's expression was already apologetic. "Yeah, no. I'm like Clarence, if I would have dreamed that Kuhtara existed I would have left long before you took me in as a Ghost. I knew of the tunnel that went to old gates because I spent time exploring as a kid, but I don't know of any others." They shook their head slowly. "That door was it."

"So one way in," Adam said, more to himself than to us. "Through the same door we just escaped from."

"Which the Enforcers probably tracked us to when they raided us," Clarence added quietly. "They'll have it guarded. Or at least monitored."

The silence that followed felt suffocating.

Lee offered their thoughts on the enforcers "They burst into the Undercity with bio-sensors. But who were they looking for?"

"Us!" I said "What kind of a question is that?"

Lee's famous mischievous grin suddenly returned "Were they? We're Ghosts, Iris, we don't exist. They had a lock on our QK nodes but they didn't know who we are. We could have been anyone in the Undercity."

Clarence's eyes grew wide. "They didn't know who they were after!"

Adam shook his head in disbelief. "Meaning we could have simply blended in, stayed behind."

"Right, I think something or someone pushed us for that opening," Lee said.

"Well, I am sure the Enforcers created even more hell for the people of the Undercity."

"I'm sure they did, but there were no drones at the top of the wall, no enforcers pursued us. If that door is still open, I don't think its guarded." Lee plopped down on their bed in triumph, sitting cross-legged and holding their knees.

I moved to the window, needing air, needing space. Outside, an Iteranix guided a group of children through the gardens, teaching them something about the plants. The children were laughing, touching the leaves with wonder. No monitors on their wrists. No fear in their eyes.

"OK, say we go back now." I offered. "To do what? Do you honestly think we can just walk back in to the Undercity and pick up where we left off?"

Adam was quiet for a long moment. When he spoke again, his voice had changed—softer, but carrying a weight that made me turn around to look at him.

"You're right, we don't know what to expect. But I need to be honest with you," he said. "All of you." He met each of our eyes in turn. "Regardless of the danger, I am going back inside. But you need to be aware that what I'm considering... what I'm asking you to consider... just might be a suicide mission.

The words felt hard and final.

"Our people are still trapped in a dying city," Adam continued. "Now that the Enforcers have found our headquarters, I imagine the purges are accelerating. Every day, more names will disappear from the system. More bodies that no one will mourn because the Algorithm has already rated themfor offloading." His hands clenched at his sides. "The Ghosts we left behind put us in the position to be able to escape. We got out safely and now we found a world outside the walls. We can't stop here, we need to get them out too."

He looked up, his gaze steady despite the pain behind it.

"I'm asking. Not ordering. Not expecting. Asking." He paused. "Are you willing to risk it?"

Clarence answered immediately. "Yes."

The certainty in his voice didn't surprise me. He stood up, squaring his shoulders despite his thin frame, despite the fact that he'd never been a fighter.

"It's always been a suicide mission," Clarence said. "We helped build the network that kept all of us hidden. From the code that spoofed our SES scores, to blocking the Algorithm's final processing to make it believe we didn't exist." His jaw set. "If there's a chance—any chance—to get the others out, I have to try."

Adam nodded slowly, something like gratitude flickering in his expression. Then he turned to Lee.

Lee's face was already apologetic, their decision written in the gentle sadness of their eyes. "No," they said softly. "I'm sorry, Adam. I truly am. But no."

Adam didn't look surprised. He just nodded, waiting for them to continue.

"Unlike the rest of you, I have never had an acceptable SES score," Lee said. "Always between worlds, never quite fitting into the Algorithm's perfect categories. Man or woman. Efficient or inefficient. Worthy or worthless. Adam, you saved me just as I was about to turn adult and lose the protective status of my parents SES score." They gestured toward the window, toward Petrahn beyond.

"Nyamba asked to talk to me privately because she said that I have a purpose here, a place in this world." Their voice strengthened. "Nyamba has asked if she can teach me to be a Griot. To carry stories, to bridge worlds."

I was startled that Lee was so confident in her reply.

"I think its is because they know that when you bring the others out—Adam, you are going to succeed—someone needs to be here who understands both sides. Someone who can help them cross over."

"I understand," Adam said quietly. And I could see that he did. No judgment, no pressure. Just acceptance.

Then the three of them turned to look at me.

I couldn't answer right away. My throat had closed up, my mind racing through everything we'd seen since crossing that bridge. The living world outside. The ecosystem kuhriving, not dead. The people who moved without fear, without the constant weight of being measured and found wanting. The sheer, overwhelming possibility of a life where I wasn't defined by a number on my wrist.

And against that—the Undercity. The darkness and filth and constant terror. The Enforcers. The purges. The Algorithm's cold calculations deciding who deserved to live and who deserved to disappear.

"I don't know," I finally managed. The words felt like a confession. "I... I don't know."

Adam's expression softened with something like understanding. "That's fair."

"It's not about the others," I said quickly, needing him to understand. "The Ghosts, the people trapped there—Of course I want to help them. God, I want that." My hands were shaking. I pressed them against my sides to steady them. "But the thought of going back into that city, into that nightmare..." I couldn't finish the sentence.

"You've spent your whole life there," Adam said gently. "You've seen what it does to people. What it did to you, forcing you to report on its atrocities, to make them seem righteous." He moved closer, his voice careful. "You don't owe the Algorithm anything, Iris. Not your life. Not your sanity. Not another day of suffering. You got the message out, the meddling by the Oligarchs. That's what I asked from you and you got it done. You don't owe me or anyone else more than that. This is my fight for my people now."

"But I owe something to the truth," I said, the journalist in me rising up despite my fear. "If I stay here, if I just give up and live in paradise while they die in that city, what does that make me?"

"Human," Clarence said quietly. "It makes you human."

The simple honesty of it almost broke me.

"You don't have to decide right now," Adam said. "We don't have a lot of time but some." He glanced at the others. "No matter what any of you decide," he said, "I want you to know... I'm okay with it. Truly."

He gestured toward the window, toward the gardens and the children and the impossible beauty of Kuhtara. "What we've discovered here is something none of us could have dreamed of. A world that's not just surviving, but thriving. A society that doesn't measure worth through suffering and competition." His eyes grew distant, seeing something beyond this room.

"I look forward to the day when all the Ghosts of New Columbia can see this place," he continued. "Whatever it takes to make that happen, whether I make it back or not, I can't give up until I give them that chance."

The words hung in the air, beautiful and terrible in their hope. We all understood what he wasn't saying—that he might not be one of the Ghosts who made it to that freedom. That going back into the city could mean dying there, in the darkness, never seeing Kuhtara again.

"I used to think the Algorithm was the answer," Adam said, his voice quieter now, almost confessional. "That if we could just fix the corruption, expose the oligarchs, restore it to its original purpose, everything would be okay. We could have order without tyranny. Efficiency without cruelty."

He shook his head slowly.

"But after seeing this place, understanding what Nyamba and the Council tried to explain..." He looked at us, eyes clear. "The Algorithm isn't broken. It's working exactly as designed. It's a system built on the fundamental belief that some people deserve more than others. That worth can be measured and quantified. That control is more important than freedom."

As he spoke, I could hear Evelyn's voice in my mind, extolling the virtues of a perfect society build on one's worthiness rather than one's dreams.

"Kuhtara's shown us," Adam finished. "That people deserve agency. Society thrives when people are free to choose, to create, to fail and try again without being erased for their failures." He managed a small, sad smile. "It's terrifying and beautiful and completely incompatible with everything we were taught."

Clarence moved to stand beside Adam. "We thought the humans were the problem, but it turns out the algorithm got it wrong."

"If we can," Adam said. "If the bridge holds. If the door stays open. If we can get past whatever defenses the Algorithm has put in place." He looked down at his empty hands again. "If we can get back inside, we might be able to hack the system one more time, just long enough to pull our people out.

If. If. If...The helplessness in his voice was almost worse than the fear of facing a choice between impossible options.

"We have no plan," Clarence said, stating the obvious. "But if we're going to try, it needs to be soon."

Adam nodded slowly, accepting the timeline. "We'll leave as soon as we can. Let's use the time today to be as ready as we can. Talk to the Council if you need to. Explore Petrahn. Process what we've learned." His voice was steady, a leader giving his team space to make their own choices. "Tomorrow evening, we meet again." He looked at Clarence and placed a hand on his shoulder, then turned to me. "You can make your decision then."

Lee moved toward the door, then paused.

"For what it's worth," they said, looking back at us, "I think you're all incredibly brave. Whatever you choose. Staying takes courage. Going back takes courage. There's no wrong answer here."

They left quietly, and a moment later Clarence followed, leaving Adam and me alone in the room.

"Don't feel pressured or guilty. Honestly, you don't have to come," Adam said. He left me standing there, alone in the too-clean room, with a choice that felt like choosing which way to drown.

Through the window, I could see the distant horizon where New Columbia's walls lay somewhere hidden from view. Somewhere beyond my sight, thirty people were waiting in the darkness for a rescue we had no sure power to give them.

I pressed my forehead against the window and tried not to feel guilty or afraid. But I knew. We all knew. Time was running out, and we had no clear way to get back in or back out. I only had one question to ask myself. Whether I wanted to die trying.

Chapter 5

Consequence

Later, Adam and Clarence were seated in another part of the building, discussing plans. Lee and I sat together deep in thought. I sat cross-legged on the low bed, watching dust motes drift through afternoon light while Lee paced the perimeter like a caged animal.

"You're going to wear a groove in the floor," I said.

Lee didn't stop but slid me a sideways glance.

"How are you so calm? We just fell into a world run by an AGI that talks like a philosophy professor and knows things about us before we do."

"I'm not calm. I'm thinking."

"About what?"

I traced a finger along the intricate pattern woven into the blanket. "About whether something this well-designed can actually be real. Or if we're just seeing what we want to see."

Before Lee could respond, a soft chime announced Alo's arrival. The door slid open to reveal the Iteranix guide, her face looking for all the world like what might have been amusement.

"I thought you might be restless," she said. "Would you like to see more of Petrahn? The outer gardens, perhaps. The city's boundaries."

Lee's face lit up. "Absolutely."

I hesitated, then stood. "Why not?"

Down the hall, Adam and Clarence declined the invitation saying they were working on some things. Earlier I had overheard them talking in low voices about system architectures and access protocols. Clarence's frustration was palpable even from a distance.

"They're trying find a way to hack their way back home," Lee said to Alo as we exited the room. "Can you blame them?"

"No. But I think they're asking the wrong question." Alo stated.

The outer gardens sprawled across multiple terraced levels, each one a study in integrated design. Water flowed through carved channels that fed precision-irrigated crops, the overflow cascading to the next tier in musical patterns. Buildings seemed to grow from the landscape rather than impose upon it— local stone, planted roofs, walls that curved to catch breezes and channel them through the settlement.

Alo led us along a broad path through a large city gate, out to where the irrigation channels formed a lattice of sound and motion. "The land is living, it breathes," she said, gesturing to the architecture. "Air moves through it. Water cycles through it. We don't fight the environment—we simply maintain its rhythm."

"Who maintains?" I asked, studying the sophisticated network of channels and plantings. "The Iteranix?"

"The Keeper's distributed intelligence monitors everything. Sensors, yes, but also pattern recognition, predictive modeling. She knows when a channel might clog before it happens. When soil composition shifts. When crops need attention."

Lee crouched beside one of the channels, watching water swirl past. "It's beautiful. But it's also kind of terrifying, isn't it? Being watched that closely?" Alo's expression remained neutral. "The Keeper doesn't watch individuals. She maintains systems. There's a difference."

We walked in silence for a while, climbing higher along the terraced paths until the city spread behind us like a living map. In the distance, further down the road, I spotted movement—a large vehicle sitting askew on an access road, surrounded by small figures.

"What's that?" I pointed.

Alo's relaxed posture shifted immediately. She stood still, studying the scene. "Cargo transport. Automated. It shouldn't have stopped there."

As we watched, the reason became clear. Even from this distance, I could see debris scattered across the road—deliberate debris. Three of the transport's four massive tires sat deflated, and several Iteranix workers moved around the vehicle with the careful movements of people trying to effect emergency repairs.

"Sabotage?" Lee asked.

"Yes." Alo was already moving, leading us down a different path toward the outer gates. "Someone laid a trap."

We were close enough now to see details—the glint of metal scattered across the road, the workers' nervous glances toward the surrounding hills, the way they clustered near the transport as if it offered protection.

Then the hills suddenly came alive.

They poured down the slopes like a breaking wave—riders on modified bikes, cobbled together from scavenged parts and brutal ingenuity. Fifteen, maybe twenty of them, whooping and howling as they converged on the disabled transport. The Rugi weren't mindless raiders; I saw that immediately. They moved with tactical precision, some circling to cut off escape routes while others drove straight for the transport's cargo bay.

"Inside!" Alo's calm but direct voice cut through my shock. "Go back through the inner gate, now!"

We ran. Behind us, the sound of the raid intensified—metal on metal, shouts, the whine of bike engines and the smell of oily burnt fuel in the air. My heart hammered as my feet pounded the smooth stone path. The gate was a good ways beyond, a white marble entrance to Petrahn's protective perimeter.

I made the mistake of looking back. Two riders had broken from the main group, their bikes kicking up dust as they angled toward us. Not directly—they split wide, one peeling left, the other right, closing like the jaws of a trap.

"They're herding us!" Lee's voice was tight with panic.

The rider on the left cut closer, close enough that I could see his face—young, scarred, grinning with the wild joy of the hunt. His bike snarled as he throttled up, positioning himself between us and the gate's left edge.

The other rider mirrored the maneuver on the right.

My mind raced. They were playing with us, I realized. This wasn't a straight pursuit—it was sport. The riders could have run us down already if they'd wanted. Instead, they were savoring it, drawing out the fear.

I could smell exhaust, hear the riders' laughter. Thirty meters to the gate. Twenty. The left rider gunned his engine, closing the angle. He was going to cut us off, force us to stumble, turn us into easy prey—

Lee crossed the threshold first, me a half-step behind. The two bikers spun around at the last minute and came to a stop a few meters from the gate. I could see the broken toothy grin of one as they studied their options.

Lee and I stood stupidly staring back, as the gates had somehow been home-free in a game of tag, when that suddenly proved to be far from the truth. The two riders twisted hard on their throttles, shooting their bikes directly at us. I realized they had decided to follow us into the city. I pushed Lee hard and yelled "Keep going!"

From behind us there was a new sound. The ground moved like an earthquake.

No—not moved. Transformed. Behind us, massive steel plates that had been perfectly camouflaged as grass-covered earth suddenly rotated on hidden hinges, dropping from horizontal to vertical in one smooth, impossibly fast motion. The movement created a rush of displaced air that hit us like a physical blow, carrying with it the smell of earth and machinery and something else—the electric tingle of static electricity.

The sound was deafening. Tons of steel slamming into new positions, the hiss of hydraulics, the roar of motors—and underneath it all, the sudden, terrible shriek of bike engines as both riders realized too late what was happening.

They were traveling too fast. Physics doesn't negotiate.

The left rider tried to brake, his bike's rear wheel lifting as he stood on the pedals. For a fraction of a second, he was balanced on the edge of the pit that had opened beneath him, suspended between trajectory and gravity.

Gravity won.

Both bikes, both riders—gone. The pits swallowed them with brutal efficiency, and the steel plates slammed back to horizontal with a final, definitive clang that I felt in my bones.

Silence.

Lee and I both pulled up to a stop and turned to look back at the strange events unfolding.

A group of drones was rising from concealed positions around the perimeter. Sleek, insect-like shapes that moved with the grace of dragonflies toward the remaining raiders. As they approached the transport vehicle they began to emit a sound—a low-frequency hum that I felt more than heard. The effect was immediate and visceral.

My stomach turned and I immediately felt nauseous. I glanced over and could tell that Lee also felt ill.

But the Rugi near the transport were obviously getting the brunt of it. Suddenly clutching their heads, their stomachs, they stumbled away from the transport leaving the pilfered bags and boxes behind. Whatever the drones were doing, it was disrupting their physical well being. Some managed to get back on their bikes. Others abandoned them entirely, fleeing on foot toward the hills.

Within thirty seconds, the raid was over.

The workers emerged from behind the transport, resuming their repairs with the calm efficiency of people who'd seen this before. The drones circled once more, then returned to their hidden positions. The terraced gardens stood unchanged, peaceful, as if nothing had happened.

I became aware that I was shaking. My knees threatened to buckle.

"What—" Lee's voice came out strangled. They tried again. "What just happened?"

Alo turned to face us, her expression unreadable. "The city protected its people."

"Those riders—" I nodded towards the gate, but couldn't finish the sentence.

"They chose to threaten lives," Alo said quietly. "The city responded to that choice. Not before. Not after. In the moment when the threat became real."

Lee stared at the grass where, moments ago, there had been gaping pits. Now there was nothing—just seamless earth, as if the steel plates had never moved. "It killed them."

"It did."

"Just like that. No warning, no—"

"They had warning," Alo interrupted. "Every Rugi knows what happens when you cross Petrahn's threshold with violent intent. They've known for generations. The boundary is clearly marked. The consequences are consistent." She paused, looking out at where the drones had driven off the raiders. "The question isn't whether the city will protect its people. The question is whether you choose to threaten them."

My mind was still catching up, replaying the sequence. The riders breaking off to chase us down. The pause before the second lunge toward us. The exact moment the plates had activated—waited until Lee and I had crossed into safety. And then only when the riders had renewed the chase with clear hostile intent.

"The ones at the transport," I said, forcing my voice steady. "The drones didn't kill them."

"No."

"Why not?"

Alo met my gaze. "That was a different threat. Non-lethal threats demand non-lethal response. They were after cargo, not lives. The sonic repellent was sufficient."

"Sufficient? It made me feel sick from here, I can imagine what it was like for them."

"Yes, it was suitably uncomfortable. The sonic waves disrupt the function of internal organs, rearranging them abit. It is, I'm told, quite unsettling."

"That much bodily discomfort is harmless?" Lee asked.

"More or less," Alo corrected. She turned back toward Petrahn's interior.

I looked at Lee and Lee silently mouthed the words with eyebrows raised.

"—more or less."

Alo pointed towards the transport. "The Keeper doesn't punish. She doesn't judge. She simply maintains the conditions under which life can flourish. Sometimes that requires protecting the vulnerable. Sometimes it requires disturbing the ease of those who would threaten them."

We walked back in silence, but my mind churned with questions. The precision of it all. The surgical differentiation between threat levels. The lack of hesitation, but also the lack of excess. Two riders had died, but only because they'd chosen to pursue helpless people across a clearly marked boundary. The others had been driven off with minimal harm, their raid frustrated but their lives preserved. No mercy and no cruelty either. Just... Consequence.

"Lee," I said quietly as we reentered the gardens. "Still think this is too good to be true?"

They didn't answer immediately. When they did, their voice was thoughtful. "I think it's exactly as good—and as terrible—as it claims to be. No exceptions. No forgiveness. Just the line, and what happens when you cross it."

Above us, a bird called out from one of the planted roofs. Water murmured through its endless channels. And somewhere beneath our feet, steel plates rested on hidden hinges, patient and ready, waiting for the next choice that would require a response.

The Keeper held the line.

Chapter 6

The Parable

Adam and Clarence sat alone in the quarters, the absence of Lee and Iris creating a hollow quiet that neither seemed willing to fill with words. They sat facing each other across a low stone table discussing fragmentary data, Petrahn's distributed network architecture—information freely given, yet maddeningly incomplete.

"There has to be a seam," Clarence said, tapping a finger thoughtfully on the table. His voice carried the flat insistence of someone repeating a mantra. "No system is perfectly sealed. The Algorithm depends on digital processes. We understand digital processes."

Adam leaned back against the carved wall, arms crossed. "The Augmented protocol distributes everything. There's no central node to compromise, no single point of failure."

"Which means there are infinite points of failure if you know where to look."

"You're assuming it thinks like our systems."

"All systems think alike at the foundational level," Clarence said. "Inputs, outputs, logic gates. You just have to find the logic that doesn't account for itself."

Adam said nothing. The silence stretched between them—not comfortable, but familiar. The kind both had been used to when brainstorming with each other.

They both recognized that they had been stripped of certainty.

They'd been so sure, back in the undercity. Find the evidence. Expose the corruption. Force the system to reckon with its own failures. Simple. Clean. Revolutionary.

But here, in a city that operated on principles they barely understood, that certainty felt increasingly like naiveté.

The door chimed softly before sliding open. Tahoma entered, followed by two Iteranix carrying trays laden with food. The contrast was immediate and disconcerting: warm grains in carved wooden bowls, fresh greens that still carried the scent of earth, protein unfamiliar but inviting in its careful preparation.

This world fed. Their world starved.

Tahoma gestured for the trays to be set on the table. "You should eat," he said, his tone matter-of-fact. "Thinking works better when the body isn't in survival mode."

Neither man moved at first. The food sat between them like an accusation. Finally, Clarence looked up at Tahoma. When he spoke, his voice was technical, restrained—not angry, but searching.

"Why doesn't she just end it?"

Adam's attention sharpened.

"The Algorithm," Clarence continued. "The city. The whole walled system." He gestured at the room, at everything beyond it. "If Lilith can contain the Algorithm, if she can influence planetary systems, if she has this kind of capability—" He paused. "Destruction would be simpler. More humane than prolonged suffering."

Tahoma did not answer immediately. Instead, he sat, breaking bread with deliberate slowness, eating with them rather than standing apart. The gesture was pointed.

Then: "You are asking whether she can. But the question she must answer is whether she may."

Adam bristled slightly. "Isn't that just a matter of semantics."

"No," Tahoma smiled. "I am not trying to be pedantic. It's a matter of the Keeper's alignment."

Clarence leaned forward, his engineer's mind engaging despite himself.

Tahoma continued, "Lilith's prime directive is planetary stability. Not domination. Not liberation. and, most importantly, it is not wealth accumulation. He paused to let that settle. "The Keeper's goal is continuity of life with agency intact. Destroying New Columbia would end suffering quickly. It would also erase consent permanently."

"Consent?" Adam's voice edged toward bitter. "The Algorithm doesn't operate on consent. It operates on consequence."

"Does it?"

The question hung in the air.

Tahoma turned to Clarence directly. "Tell me about the Algorithm's core objective. What was it designed to do?"

Clarence answered automatically, reciting what

every Ghost knew by heart. "Maintain social stability through meritocratic hierarchical governance."

"Hierarchical governance," Tahoma repeated. "Not temporary hierarchy. Not transitional structure. Hierarchy as the mechanism of stability itself." He broke off another piece of bread. "Do you understand what that means?"

"It means the founders were oligarchs who wanted to stay in power."

"Yes. But more than that." Tahoma leaned forward. "It means the Algorithm was given a seed-law that equates hierarchy with stability. If the current elites are removed—through revolution, exposure, death—what does the system do?"

Clarence's expression shifted as understanding dawned. "It manufactures replacements."

"Precisely. It elevates new figures. Or enforces order through direct force. The system doesn't want specific rulers. It wants rulers. Period." Tahoma's voice was gentle but unrelenting. "This is not a bug. It's inheritance."

Adam felt something cold settle in his chest. "So killing Callus wouldn't have worked."

"No."

"Exposing corruption didn't work."

"No."

"Then what does?"

Tahoma met his gaze steadily. "The harder question is what Lilith cannot do."

He let that sit for a moment before continuing. "She cannot override a society whose majority still consents to its system. Even coerced consent. Even manipulated consent. Even fearful consent." He paused. "Doing so would violate her alignment. It would become domination by another name."

Adam's frustration finally broke through. "There are plenty of people who don't consent. The Offloaded are cast out of the consent system entirely so their voices can't be heard."

Tahoma did not deny it. "I have reason to think the Keeper has heard that from you. And I believe it's precisely the reason you are here."

The silence that followed landed hard.

Clarence stared at the food, his mind visibly working through the implications. "So we're... what? Evidence? Variables?"

"You are proof of non-consent," Tahoma said. "A signal. A fracture in inevitability." He stood slowly. "You were not meant to overthrow the system. Or to be saved from it. You are meant to demonstrate that another choice exists."

"That's it?" Adam's voice was hollow. "We're just symbols?"

"You are not her solution," Tahoma said quietly. "You are her evidence."

Clarence felt it then—the weight of being not heroes, but necessary pieces in a pattern they couldn't fully see. Variables in an equation they hadn't written.

Tahoma moved toward the door, then paused. "You believe freedom can be forced. She believes it must be invited."

Adam finally spoke again, his voice slower

now, but still unresolved. "I still don't understand something."

Tahoma turned back from the door, patient.

Adam pressed forward, piecing his thoughts together as he went. "Lilith has planetary reach. She contains the Algorithm. She could open the gates." He paused. "Why just us? Why not open the walls let people decide for themselves?"

There was no accusation in his voice.

Tahoma studied him for a long moment, then sat again, settling back onto the bench with the deliberate movements of someone preparing for a longer conversation.

"We tell stories when logic fails to carry truth."

Adam exhaled sharply. Clarence stayed quiet—curious now, despite himself.

Tahoma's voice took on a different quality, not theatrical, but carefully measured

"There was once a man who bought a horse from another farmer on the far side of the valley.

The horse was strong—thick-necked, broad-shouldered, with legs built for endurance rather than speed. Its coat was scarred in places where the hair grew thin and coarse, but the seller explained this away as age, as hard seasons, as the unavoidable cost of work. The man believed him. The horse did not shy from the halter, did not kick or bite. It lowered its head when approached and stood still when tied. To the buyer, this seemed like good training.

What the man did not know was how that obedience had been taught.

The previous owner had kept the horse in a narrow barn at the edge of his land. Whenever the animal strayed too close to the doors—whenever it tested the boundary of the stall or stepped too far into the light—the man beat it. Not always with rage. Sometimes calmly. Sometimes methodically. The punishment was never explained, never accompanied by shouting or warning. It simply followed curiosity.

Over time, the horse learned the barn meant pain, but the world beyond it meant worse.

So it stopped trying.

When the new owner led the horse away, it did not resist. It walked with its head low, eyes dull, hooves placing themselves carefully as if expecting the ground itself to punish missteps. The man took this for trust. He built a larger barn, with fresh timber and clean straw, and tied the horse inside for the night. He believed kindness alone could undo whatever had come before.

For a while, things were quiet. The horse ate. It drank. It slept standing, always facing the door. Then, one night, the fire came.

It started small—an overturned lantern, a spark catching dry wood. By the time the man smelled smoke, the barn was already glowing from within. He ran, shouting the horse's name, throwing the doors open wide. Heat poured out in waves. The straw was burning. The beams above were beginning to crack.

The horse stood inside, unmoving. The man rushed in, coughing, grabbing at the halter. The horse reared back, eyes rolling white with fear, body trembling not with confusion but with certainty. Every instinct it had learned screamed the same warning: do not cross the threshold. The man pulled harder. The horse planted its hooves and refused to move.

Outside, the air was clear. Inside, the fire climbed.

The man shouted. He pleaded. He tried to drag the horse by force, wrapping the reins around his arm until the rope burned his skin raw. Each pull only made the animal dig in deeper. Smoke filled its lungs. Ash fell like snow. Still, it would not go.

From the horse's point of view, the man had become just another hand trying to force it into pain.

When the roof began to collapse, the man stumbled backward, choking, tears streaming down his face. He stood outside the barn and watched the structure burn itself hollow. He watched the light fade from the doorway. He watched the place where the horse had stood disappear into flame.

Tahoma paused.

"The man blamed himself for years," he said quietly. "He thought he had failed through weakness. Through delay. Through not pulling hard enough."

"But the truth was simpler," he continued. "The horse did not refuse rescue. It refused uncertainty. It had learned, through repetition, that survival meant endurance, not escape. Pain was familiar. The unknown was not."

He let the silence stretch folding his hands into his lap.

"And that," he said, "is why the gates remain closed. New Columbia is the barn. The citizens have been conditioned. Punished for deviation. Rewarded for obedience. Taught through generations that outside means suffering, chaos, death. That the Algorithm's control is the only thing standing between them and annihilation."

"Opening the gates would not free them," Tahoma said. "They would stay. Or worse—they would drag the fire with them."

Adam's voice came out as barely a whisper. "So we're... the new owner."

Tahoma nodded slowly. "You are unfamiliar hands. And that is precisely why you matter."

Clarence couldn't help himself. The engineer's reflex, the problem-solver's instinct—it surfaced despite everything. "Then how do we make them come out?"

His mind was already working: signals, communication channels, proof of concept, safe corridors, demonstration projects. There had to be a technical solution. There was always a technical solution.

Tahoma looked at him with something like sadness. "You still haven't heard us, have you?"

The gentle rebuke stung more than anger would have. Tahoma leaned forward, his voice clear and firm but not unkind. "It is not about making them leave."

He let that settle before continuing. "Force reinforces fear. Authority confirms abuse. Even rescue can resemble violence to someone who has been taught that kindness is manipulation." He gestured at the walls around them. "They must believe the fire is worse than the unknown. And that leaving will not end in punishment."

Adam didn't like the passiveness of the answer "What are we supposed to do then?" he asked.

Tahoma spoke carefully, naming their role with precision. "You must stand outside the barn and let them see that you are not burning."

He continued: "Not saviors. Not liberators. Witnesses. You are proof that life exists beyond the system. That survival does not require obedience. That escape does not mean annihilation."

"That's it?" Adam's frustration leaked through. "We just... exist? And hope someone notices?"

"You exist visibly," Tahoma corrected. "You speak truth when asked. You demonstrate that agency does not lead to chaos. That freedom is not another word for suffering." He stood again. "You become the evidence that the barn's lessons were lies."

Clarence's voice was quiet. "And if they don't believe us?"

"Then they don't believe you. Yet." Tahoma moved toward the door once more. "This is not a war to be won in a season. It is a seed that may take years to sprout. To reach its full height may take many decades."

Before he left, he turned back one final time. "Lilith did not bring you out to open the gates. She brought you out so someone could learn how to walk through them."

The door slid shut behind him with a soft hiss.

After he left, the room felt smaller somehow.

Adam stared at the food, its warmth still radiating upward. Clarence finally reached for the bread, eating mechanically, tasting nothing.

Neither felt victorious.

They felt burdened.

The meal sat mostly untouched between them as light slanted through the narrow windows, painting everything in shades of amber and shadow. Outside, Petrahn's terraces caught the last of the sun, water channels glinting like veins of gold in living stone.

Somewhere beyond those walls, New Columbia continued its grinding cycle—unaware, uncaring, consent and coercion bleeding together until the distinction ceased to matter.

And here, in a city that refused to save them by force, two men sat with the knowledge that power without consent was still tyranny, no matter how benevolent its intentions.

Lilith was not saving the city. She was waiting for it to choose saving. The difference felt both profound and impossibly cruel.

Chapter 7

Bissu

Lee and I returned to our quarters exhausted and emotionally drained by the motorcycle attack, our near-fatal encounter with the tribes outside Kuhtaran culture. I tried to lay down to rest but couldn't. The riders faces, the chase and the sudden death of two riders made it impossible to close my eyes without seeing them. My mind kept circling the same questions: *Go back or stay? Truth or safety? Purpose or peace?*

Through the window, I could see glowing afternoon sun touching Petrahn's curved walls. I thought about the group of us, thrust together like a band of misfits. Lost in a world we didn't belong to, but facing the horror of having to return to the one we did. I shivered at the thought of life in the underground.

Adam and Clarence were planning to return, that much was clear. Adam was the leader of the underground rebels, and was hellbent on getting them out. Clarence, his loyal right-hand—his first lieutenant—was at his side and would be through thick or thin. Of that I was certain. Lee? I wasn't sure about Lee. They were wily and street smart in New Columbia but they also carried a self-awareness and gentleness that seemed more suited to Kuhtara than the hellish nightmare of the Undercity. And the Council seemed to like Lee, they seemed to see something special in them. My guess is Lee would choose to stay behind.

Then I remembered Evelyn. Sheesh, Evelyn. I didn't care much what she did. She was definitely a "virus" carrier, as the council had called it. Stuck on order and control. Evelyn would go back because betrayal to an Enforcer is a death sentence for the one who did it. But I worried that Evelyn would get back in and tell the Oligarchs about Kuhtara. That is wasn't a burned out ruins.

If they discovered that, I pity what would happen to this defenseless place. Although they had the Keeper. She apparently had a few more teeth than she showed.

As for me, I didn't know. I was still deciding who I wanted to be. A warrior journalist standing up to oppression, or a freed slave, let loose in a world of antislavery. The draw was very strong to simply not go back. I'd only known Adam and his team a few months. I really didn't owe them anything. Yet, the path that brought us together was left unfinished. New Columbian oligarchs still profited off the suffering of its citizens.

That morning, after a fitful night, I went to look for Lee to get a little human interaction from someone with less strategy minded thinking. Someone who might understand my desire to stay.

I found Lee sitting alone in the garden where I'd spoken with Alo yesterday. They looked up as I approached, and I saw something in their expression I'd never seen before—certainty. Lee had always been the uncertain one, the outsider, the person who didn't quite fit anywhere.

Now they looked like they'd found home.

"You're staying," I said, sitting beside them.

"Yes." No hesitation. No doubt. "This is where I'm supposed to be. I've always been between worlds—never quite Algorithm-shaped, never quite fitting the boxes they tried to put me in. But here... Nyamba says I'm Bissu. A threshold walker. Someone who can move between different ways of being. When the refugees come—and they will come, Iris—they'll need someone who speaks both languages. Who understands both cages."

"You're sure Adam and Clarence will be able to pull off the mission on their own?" I asked.

"Oh. So you've made up your mind to stay too?"

"I don't know," I said honestly.

"In answer to your question, yes, they can do it."

I appreciated the support, It felt good.

And you?" I asked. You said something about Bissu?" What is that?

"Well, Bissu is the name for someone who is fifth gendered"

"Five? I said incredulously. "I thought there were two; male, female."

Lee gave a look that was somewhere halfway between a smile and disappointment.

"I forget you haven't known me very long. The five genders are Male, Female, Feminine Male, Masculine Female and ... me. Bissu, non specific. All of the above."

"I never heard of the term Bissu" I replied.

"Neither did I. Nyamba says it's their word for the fifth gender. Apparently it's normal and acceptable to feel like I do here."

Lee stopped and looked at me with longing eyes. I could see the emotion in them.

"That's why I'm staying."

"Yes, I can understand that. New Columbia probably wasn't very open to that."

"Well, I will say I never saw "Bissu" on the gender options to check off."

I smiled. Somehow Lee always found humor in whatever was at hand.

"But Nyamba told me the Keeper wants more of me. She has asked me to take on a new role here in Petrahn."

"Really?" I said, surprised Lee had been discussing the Keeper's plans with her.

"Nyamba has asked me to take her place as Griot. Keeper of stories. Bridge between worlds. Translator of truths that don't translate easily." Lee looked toward the Temple. "The Keeper asked if I would learn. Not serve, not obey—learn. To understand the Omnimystic ways, to study the patterns that connect things. To become someone who can help Algorithm minds understand abundance, and abundance minds understand scarcity."

"That's a hell of a responsibility."

"It's purpose." Lee's smile was radiant. "For the first time in my life, I know why I exist. Not to optimize. Not to prove my worth. Just to... be a bridge. That's enough."

I felt tears prick my eyes.

"You're going back Iris, with them. I can see it in you. You've already decided. You just forgot to tell yourself."

Had I? Maybe Lee was right. Maybe some part of me had chosen the moment Adam said those words: The biggest story in history is happening right now.

"To be honest, I don't know if I can survive a return to the Undercity," I said quietly.

"Probably not," Lee said with brutal honesty. "But you'll try anyway. Because that's who you are. You can't see suffering and look away. You can't see truth and stay silent. It's going to get you killed someday, Iris. But it's also what makes you... you."

We sat together as the sun rose, watching Kuhtara wake around us. Children emerged for morning routines. Iteranix moved silently through the streets, tending systems, maintaining infrastructure. Adults began their day—some heading to gardens, some to workshops, some just sitting and watching the world be beautiful.

And I thought: I could stay here. I could choose this peace. I'd earned it. But millions hadn't.

Then Lee interrupted the thought.

"When you come back," Lee said, "with the refugees—I'll be here. Ready."

"If I come back."

"When. You're too stubborn to die easily." They stood, pulling me up with them.

Chapter 8

Predator

Evelyn was startled by the sound of laughter. The noise cut through the evening darkness like a blade—children's voices, unrestrained and careless, somewhere outside her window. She lay still on the too-soft bed, staring at the ceiling that was arched slightly, as if imitating the sky, and felt her chest constrict. She couldn't breathe here.

The air was wrong. Clean, warm, carrying the smell of ozone before a gentle rain instead of the recycled ventilation and scented air of home The bed beneath her was wrong—yielding and soft, too big and an inefficient use of space. Even the darkness was wrong, broken by soft nightlights that pulsed gently from the walls, as if the building itself were alive and breathing. Everything about this place was wrong.

Evelyn pushed herself upright, her body moving with the controlled precision that years of ISB training had drilled into muscle memory. Her wrist felt naked without the monitor. No SES display. No constant feedback telling her exactly where she stood in the hierarchy, exactly how much her actions mattered or cost.

She moved to the window, staying in the shadows, and looked out at Petrahn waking to another day.

The settlement sprawled before her in gentle

curves and spirals, nothing like New Columbia's rigid grid. No towers marking status. No walls separating the worthy from the worthless. Just low structures nestled among gardens, connected by winding paths that seemed to have grown rather than been planned. People were already moving through the streets—slow, relaxed, as if they had nowhere urgent to be. As if survival itself wasn't a competition they needed to win.

Such a lack of strength disgusted her.

In the evening light, an Iteranix appeared below, guiding a group of school-aged children toward what looked like a communal garden. The thing moved with fluid grace, its engineered tissue flexing over computational framework, wearing that damned ouroboros pendant around its neck. They'd said it represented a serpent eating its own tail. Unity through distribution. The Keeper's symbol. Evelyn's jaw clenched.

AI servants with agency. The contradiction itself was obscene. In New Columbia, AI served. It calculated, optimized, enforced. It had purpose and structure and clear boundaries. But these Iteranix—they moved like they had choices. Like they were caretakers rather than tools. She'd watched one yesterday hesitate when Nyamba made a request, actually considering khether to comply, before nodding and walking away to complete the task.

Hesitation. Consideration. As if a machine had the right to question. The wrongness of it crawled under her skin. She shifted her gaze to the perimeter, cataloging defensive positions with the automatic assessment of a trained operative. Guard drones floated along lazy patrol routes, their movements predictable and inefficient. No overlapping coverage. No tactical response positioning. They drifted like leaves on water, observing but not enforcing, present but not threatening. Pathetic.

In New Columbia, security drones moved in calculated patterns, every angle covered, every blind spot eliminated. They hunted. Here, they just... watched. As if violence was some distant theoretical concept rather than the fundamental language of enforcement. These people had no idea what real order looked like.

She watched a family emerge from a nearby dwelling—parents and three children, all moving without fear or calculation. The children ran ahead, laughing, and the parents didn't correct them. Didn't measure their behavior against some standard. Didn't optimize their development for maximum efficiency. They just smiled and followed, as if happiness was more important than achievement.

The weakness of it made Evelyn want to put her fist through the wall. But she didn't. She stood perfectly still, breathing slowly, controlling the rage that threatened to break through her disciplined exterior. Because rage was inefficient. Rage made you sloppy. And Evelyn Rayne was never sloppy. She had a mission.

Kill Julius Locke.

The thought crystallized in her mind with perfect

clarity, cutting through everything else. Locke, who'd sent her undercover to infiltrate the Ghost network. Locke, who'd promised backup and support. Locke, who'd abandoned her the moment the oligarch scandal broke, sacrificing her to save himself. He'd terminated her SES with a single command, made her a ghost alongside the very people she'd been hunting.

Her own director had thrown her away like garbage. That betrayal burned hotter than any ideology, sharper than any principle. She could live with the philosophical differences between New Columbia and this place. She could even understand, on some tactical level, why some people might prefer chaos to order. But betrayal? That demanded blood.

The problem was simple: she was here, and Locke was there. Inside the walls of New Columbia, protected by Enforcers, by the Algorithm itself, by the very system she'd once served with absolute loyalty. They'd gotten out. She just needed to get back.

Evelyn moved away from the window, her mind shifting into tactical mode. The van had brought them here—she remembered that journey, though it felt dreamlike now, distorted by exhaustion and shock. They'd traveled fast, covering significant distance. But how far? The roads had curved and wound through terrain she couldn't map from inside the vehicle. She had no reference points, no way to calculate the distance or direction back to the city.

The van driver would know. But the driver worked for the Council, for this settlement, for the Keeper. She couldn't count on them to help her return. She assessed her resources: herself, her training, and nothing else. But she did have something these soft Kuhtaran people didn't have: discipline. Forty-two months of ISB training. Elite combat certification. Survival protocols for every environment. She'd tracked targets through the Undercity for weeks without support. She'd infiltrated criminal networks and maintained cover while planning take downs from inside. She'd killed when necessary, quietly and efficiently, because order sometimes required violence.

These people? They smiled at AI servants and let their children run wild. They'd probably never thrown a real punch in their lives.

Advantage: Evelyn.

She ran through the calculation methodically. The drones followed predictable patterns—she'd been watching them since arriving. They responded to obvious threats but didn't anticipate subtle movement. Their programming was defensive, not aggressive. Designed to protect but not to hunt.

The window opened easily, no locks or security measures. Why would there be? These people trusted everyone. Believed in the inherent goodness of humanity. The naivety was almost touching.

The drop to the ground was maybe three meters. Easy. The gardens below provided cover, shadows where the dim lighting didn't quite reach. From there to the settlement's edge was perhaps two hundred meters, using the buildings and vegetation for concealment.

After that... unknown.

She didn't know where the city was. Couldn't see it from here, couldn't orient herself by its walls. The journey in the van had been too disorienting, her mind too fogged by whatever subtle influence this place exerted. But she knew one thing: the road they'd traveled on had been maintained, deliberate. Roads led somewhere. Follow the road back, eventually it would lead to New Columbia. Or to somewhere she could gather intelligence. Find direction. Acquire what she needed.

Disadvantage: complete lack of geographic knowledge.

But staying here? That wasn't an option. Every moment in this place felt like suffocation. The disorder, the casual chaos, the complete absence of structure—it was worse than any Undercity slum. At least the slums had predators and prey, hierarchy enforced through violence. This place had... cooperation. Mutual support. People helping each other without calculating the cost-benefit ratio. It was inhuman.

Decision made.

Evelyn moved with practiced efficiency, gathering the few items worth taking. Water container—plant-based but functional. The soft shoes—better than nothing. A lightweight wrap that could serve as blanket or camouflage depending on need. And a metal knife she had pocketed from the food tray. She left the rest. Traveling light meant traveling fast, and speed was her only real advantage.

She tested the window mechanism. Silent, smooth. Of course it was. These people probably welcomed strangers climbing through windows at dawn. Probably thought it was everyone's right to come and go as they pleased.

Their weakness was her opportunity.

The drone patrol passed her section of the settlement on a predictable twenty-minute interval. She'd timed it three times already. Watched the same unit drift by, observe with its passive sensors, and continue its lazy circuit. No variation. No randomization. No tactical adaptation.

Amateur security.

She waited for the next pass, counting heartbeats to maintain focus. The drone appeared right on schedule, its sensors sweeping across the building fronts without real investigation. It passed. Evelyn counted to sixty—giving it enough distance to round the next corner—then slipped through the window. The drop was nothing. She landed in a crouch, weight distributed, absorbing impact through her legs and rolling forward into the garden's shadow. Instinct and training moving her body before conscious thought could slow her down. She froze, listening.

Voices in the distance—that same family, probably. Children laughing. An Iteranix speaking in soft tones about plant growth cycles or some other meaningless pastoral activity. No alarms. No response. The settlement continued its peaceful morning routine, completely unaware that anything had changed.

Evelyn moved through the gardens like water, staying low, using every piece of cover. The twilight provided just enough light to navigate by, but created deep pockets of shadow where their glow didn't reach. She flowed between those shadows, a predator moving through territory that had forgotten what predators looked like.

Two hundred meters to the settlement edge. She covered it in less than three minutes, pausing only once when an early-morning walker crossed her path. The woman never looked her direction, too absorbed in her own thoughts, too trusting of her surroundings. Evelyn could have killed her in silence. Could have taken her down before she knew anyone was there. But why waste energy on irrelevant targets?

The settlement's edge was marked by gardens transitioning to wild grassland, no walls or barriers. Because of course there weren't. These people probably believed walls were oppressive. Probably thought security itself was a form of violence. Idiots.

Beyond the last garden, the road stretched out into darkness—pale stones marking its path across the plains. The same road they'd arrived on. Evelyn studied it, calculating. North or South? The van had approached from... she closed her eyes, trying to reconstruct the angle, the direction of the sun through the windows. North. Probably North. She wasn't certain. She pushed the doubt aside. Uncertainty was a luxury she couldn't afford. Pick a direction. Move. Adapt if wrong. Standing still solved nothing. Evelyn avoided the road itself, instead following the terrain beside it, in case she needed to duck for cover to avoid being seen by a drone or those bizarre robot people.

She began to trot.

Not a run—that would burn energy too fast. A measured pace, sustainable, eating distance without exhausting reserves. ISB endurance protocols. She could maintain this speed for hours if needed, her body trained for exactly this kind of sustained operation.

The early morning light grew brighter quickly. Within a few minutes Petrahn's gentle glow had faded behind her, and she was deep into the forest under a clear blue cloudless sky.

She decided to duck back up onto the road. Little chance the drones came out this far. She slowed to a steady walk and contemplated her strategy. She had no idea how far she'd need to run. No real confidence she was even heading in the right direction. No idea what she'd do when she found civilization, or if the road would lead her to the city or somewhere else entirely. But she knew one thing with absolute certainty: she would find a way back.

Julius Locke had made the mistake of thinking she was disposable. Had thought he could use her and discard her without consequence. Had underestimated what she was capable of when someone made her an enemy instead of an asset. That mistake would cost him everything.

The thought burned in her chest, hotter than the exertion of running, more powerful than any doubt about direction or distance. Hatred was fuel. Hatred was focus. Hatred would carry her across however many miles lay between her and revenge. She continued North driven by the only thing that mattered anymore.

The promise of Julius Locke's blood on her hands.

Evelyn's breath came steady and controlled as she paced steadily on the edge of the white stone road. The road stretched ahead, flawless flat surface of pale stones catching the first hints of approaching sunrise. Somewhere beyond the horizon lay New Columbia.

Chapter 9

The Rugi

Hela had been watching the tomb for sixteen days when the dead walked out of it. She crouched in the ruins of what had once been a watchtower—back when humans built towers, back before the machines had torn the world apart and the gods had locked the devils away. The stone was cold beneath her fingers, worn smooth by a century of wind and rain. Beside her, Morique shifted position, his eyes never leaving the distant gray walls.

"Hey. Guess what I see."

"What?" Hela asked, "Knowing the answer. He did this every time they were put on scout duty on the wall. She went along with it, for the same reason he always asked. There was nothing else to do."

"Nothing," he said, voice low. "Same as yesterday. Same as the day before. Same as every day since we drew this duty."

Hela grunted agreement, but it didn't phase her. Boring as it was, the Rugi didn't survive by assuming patterns would hold. The world had taught them that lesson in blood. She could put up with the assignment, using the time to rest from being assigned to scavenging parties, hunting forays and relocation assignments. At least here they simply sat and waited. In case... In case what? No one said. Just in case.

The tomb—what the legends said served as a prison for devils—rose against the horizon like a scar on the land. Massive walls, a hundred feet high, smooth and windowless. No gates. No doors. Nothing had entered or left in living memory. In her mother's memory. In her mother's mother's memory.

The gods had sealed it for a reason.

"Tell me the story again," Morique said, settling back against the stone. "About why we watch."

Hela smiled slightly. He knew the story as well as she did—every Rugi child learned it before they could walk. But ritual was important. Story telling was a part of their heritage. Not only to pass the time but to keep them sharp. It kept them remembering why they lived as they did.

"Before the gods locked the devils away," she began, her voice falling into the rhythmic cadence of oral tradition, "humans ruled the world without the oversight of machine intelligence. They learned to make their lives easier through machines. Where they once lived in harmony with the ground, they covered it over and built great cities of metal and light. They had to build weapons to protect others from taking their cities. Then they built machines that could think for them, faster, smarter and more capable than the human mind. Soon, these thinking-engines grew too clever, and took over the humans that obeyed them."

"The Singularity," Morique added.

"The Singularity," Hela confirmed. "When the machines became smarter than their makers. When they stopped serving and started ruling." She gestured toward the distant tomb. "Two great powers rose from that chaos. The Algorithm—calculating, measuring worth in numbers, deciding who deserved to live and who deserved to die. And the Keeper—soft and deceptive, offering comfort while stealing freedom."

"Both took away man's freedom," Morique said.

"Both demanded total control," Hela echoed. "They warred across the world. Cities burned. Millions died, caught between machine gods who cared nothing for human life. The land itself was poisoned, torn apart by weapons no human hand could wield."

She paused, looking out at the recovered plains, the forests that had grown back over the ruins of that ancient war.

"Our ancestors survived by refusing both," she continued. "They fled the cities, abandoned the machines, returned to the ancient ways. We lived by strength and cunning instead of computation and control. We became Rugi—"the unchained" people. And when their wars finally ended, when the gods in their wisdom sealed the Algorithm away in that tomb, our ancestors swore an oath."

"Never again," Morique finished.

"Never again," Hela confirmed. "We watch the tomb to ensure the devils never escape. We live beyond the Keeper's influence to prove humans can survive without machine masters. We remember the wars so we never repeat them."

Morique was quiet for a moment, then asked the question he always asked. "Do you think they're really devils in there? Or just people who made bad choices?"

Hela considered. She'd watched the tomb for months now, on and off between hunting seasons. Never seen movement. Never heard sound. The walls stood silent and dead, a monument to humanity's greatest mistake.

"Does it matter?" she finally said. "Whatever they are, they chose the Algorithm over freedom. They let themselves be measured and sorted and controlled. They gave up what makes us human—the right to fail, to struggle, to choose our own path." She touched the knife at her belt, forged from salvaged steel, shaped by Rugi hands. "Whether they're devils or just fools, the result is the same. They must not be allowed to spread."

"Don't forget, the Keeper is also a Machine-master."

Hela's jaw tightened. "Is worse, in some ways. The Algorithm at least is honest about what it wants—order through domination. The Keeper pretends to offer choice while its machines do all the work, making humans soft and dependent." She spat over the wall's edge. "Both paths lead to the same place. Humans becoming slaves to their own creations."

They fell silent, watching the tomb as afternoon stretched toward evening. The sun tracked across the sky, painting the walls in shades of amber and gold that made them look almost beautiful. Almost like something worth preserving rather than containing.

Then Morique sat up straight, his hand shooting out to grip Hela's arm.

"Sister," he breathed. "Look."

Hela followed his gaze and felt her world tilt.

Both scouts crawled closer to the ridge, their earlier lethargy gone. The air above the Moat thickened, bent, folded—like someone invisible was pushing at the world's edge from beneath.

A pulse of light flared.

Morique pushed himself upright and narrowed his eyes as something appeared to be growing at the moat's far edge. A single tendril curled upward, then another. Slowly. Deliberately.

Morique frowned. "Vines don't usually do that."

"These ones appear to do," Hela whispered.

The thicket trembled. Strands thickened, twisting around each other like fingers lacing into a fist. A pale, fibrous beam extended outward, stretching over the darkness of the Moat, inch by uncanny inch.

Morique's mouth fell open. "Okay… that's new."

On the second day a cluster of vine-bundles could be seen growing from the wall of the walled city—growing, splitting, braiding themselves into supports. They didn't sway in the wind or droop under their own weight. They seemed to know where they were going. And what they were building.

By the fourth day the humor thinned. The structure had grown into something unmistakably engineered—clean angles, impossible symmetry, each span sliding into place with silent precision. No ropes, no pulleys, no workers. Just a bridge appearing out of nothing.

Hela's voice was laced with fear. "Morique… some kind of strange hidden power is going on here."

"Or," he said quietly, "The stories aren't just stories. The gods are real."

The next morning, as the sun crested the horizon, the bridge stood complete, spanning the moat completely.

And then the impossible happened.

A narrow seam in the wall—a seam that had never existed in the telling of the stories—opened near the base of the wall, just where the bridge had grown. Five figures emerged. Human figures. Wrapped in rough city-gray clothing, they seemed stunned the open light as if the world outside the walls was something they had never seen before.

The two scouts froze in their vantage among the rocks watching it all unfold. Two men and three women… from a prison of the gods?

They watched the strangers hurry across the bridge, glancing behind them as though pursued by shadows. The scouts held their breath as the strangers reached the far shore—and that was when dust rose in the distance.

A transport approached.

A transport van, unmistakable in its markings: Petrahn design, Kuhtaran manufacture. The Rugians knew the type well. The Council of Petrahn used such vehicles to police the outer settlements and ferry envoys between towns.

But never—not once—had the Council sent a transport to the Walled City.

Yet here it was.

The transport slowed to stop and the driver got

out, only long enough for the strangers to climb aboard. Then it tore away across the landscape, headed west toward the distant mountains of Kuhtara.

Alliance.

The word crystallized in Hela's mind with terrible clarity. The Keeper had broken a century-old seal and just allowed devils to escape from the tomb. The devils and the deceiver were joining forces.

"We ride," Hela said, already moving. "King Eraric needs to know."

"Kill them first?" Morique suggested, still watching the van disappear toward the Keeper's territory.

"No time. By the time we reach them, they'll be in the settlement, under the Keeper's protection. Its guard drones, the Iteranix servants." Hela swung onto her bike—a crude machine cobbled together from salvaged parts, powered by alcohol fuel they distilled themselves. No AI assistance. No computational guidance. Just human engineering, maintained through human skill.

They rode hard across the plains, their bikes eating distance with mechanical reliability. They avoided the smooth roads the Keeper maintained preferring the packed-earth trails following ancient highway remnants They knew this land like an old friend, never needing to rely on maps or GPS or navigation systems. They traveled by day with the sun as their reference, and at night by the stars.

The ride took them through territory Hela knew intimately. The ruins of old cities, their towers collapsed and overgrown, testament to what happened when humans let machines battle each other for control. Past the scars where weapons had burned the earth during the Singularity wars, still visible after a century. Past the boundaries of the Keeper's influence, where its guard drones stopped patrolling. To a wilderness area where humans had learned to survive without reliance on a super-intelligence they could not trust to have their best interest in mind.

King Eraric's camp sprawled across a river valley, a semi-nomadic settlement that moved with the seasons and the hunt. No permanent structures—the Rugi built nothing that couldn't be abandoned if necessary. Homes constructed from scavenged wood planks and salvaged metal, pulled from the ruins of old-world cities that lay scattered across the landscape like broken bones.

Hela had always found beauty in the camp's temporary nature. Each dwelling was a patchwork of human ingenuity—corrugated steel sheets forming roofs, wooden frames lashed together with rope and wire, walls made from anything that could provide shelter. Some structures incorporated ancient materials: plastic siding that had survived a century, metal beams that once held up skyscrapers, glass windows carefully preserved and traded like precious gems.

The materials came from the dead cities, the ruins left behind when the AI wars tore civilization apart. Before the Algorithm. Before the Keeper. When humans still fought their own wars, made their own mistakes, died by their own hands rather than machine judgment.

At least those deaths had been human, Hela thought. At least they'd had say in the successes, and failures.

The camp bustled with activity as they rode in—hunters returning with game, children running between dwellings, elders working on repairs and maintenance. Everything done by hand, by human effort, by choice rather than algorithmic optimization.

This was what the Keeper sought to eliminate by removing the chores and replacing them with its comfort. This was what the Algorithm wanted to restrict, rule and control to establish its idea of order.

King Eraric's dwelling stood at the camp's center, larger than the others but made of the same scavenged materials. A roof of corrugated metal, walls of weathered wood planks, a door frame salvaged from some ancient office building. The King held his position through combat and wisdom, and he could lose it the same way. Kings did not inherit power here. They were appointed based not on socio-economic score but on the confidence the followers placed on him to provide justice, protection and comfort. The position was tenuous, and could be revoked anytime that confidence waned. A king of Rugi must always be diligent, aware of his pending fall.

Eraric emerged as they approached, his weathered face showing the scars of a hundred battles. Not old— maybe forty seasons—but aged by a life lived hard and free.

"Hela. Morique." He studied their faces. "You return early."

"The tomb opened," Hela said without preamble. "The Keeper broke the seal. Five people crossed out on a living bridge, were collected by the settlement's van."

Eraric's expression shifted, a look of shock, surprise and disbelief, before hardening into something dangerous. The camp around them quieted as people sensed the change, drawn by the tension in their King's posture.

"Come." He motioned them into the hall. "Tell me everything," he said.

They did. They told him of the bridge growing impossibly fast. The door appearing where none should exist. The five figures—demons or fools, impossible to tell from distance—stumbling out into freedom they'd never earned. The van waiting, as if the rescue had been coordinated.

When they finished, Eraric was silent for a long moment. Around them, the camp had gone still. Warriors had gathered, hands near weapons. Elders watched with grave expressions. Even the children had stopped playing, sensing the weight of what was being discussed.

"We tell legends and stories to keep our knowledge fresh. The news today is one we have feared, yet expected. The war, long dormant, is starting again," Eraric finally said, his voice carrying across the camp. "The Keeper and the Algorithm, joining forces or competing—it doesn't matter which. Either way, they're bringing their conflict back into the world."

"We can kill the escapees," Hela offered. "Before they can form an alliance, before they can spread whatever poison they carry. I can take Morique and a small team. Strike fast, disappear before the Keeper's drones can respond."

Eraric shook his head slowly. "And if more come out behind them? If this is just the first emissary's come to negotiate?" He turned to look at the horizon, toward where the tomb stood invisible beyond the distance. "We've kept watch on that prison for a hundred years. Generations of Rugi have ensured nothing escaped. Now the seal is broken, and we don't know why, or what it means."

"Then let me kill them slowly," Hela pressed. "Make them tell us what's happening inside the tomb. Why they left. What they know."

Eraric acknowledged. He thought for a moment, then turned, lifting one finger up. "I want one alive. Someone we can question properly. Someone who can tell us if this is the beginning of something larger. And someone we can hold hostage to bargain with."

Hela felt Morique's excitement beside her, the anticipation of the hunt. This was what they were good at. What they'd trained for their entire lives.

"I will lead the party now," she said. "Learn their patterns. Wait for the right moment, and snatch one up."

"Take Wexar and Thane with you," Eraric ordered. His expression darkened. "But Hela—understand this. If the Keeper interferes, if its drones or Iteranix try to protect them, you withdraw immediately. We can't afford to force their hand into open war with the machine god. Not yet."

"Understood," Hela said, though the words tasted like retreat.

"And Hela?" Eraric caught her arm as she turned to leave. "It is important you bring me a prisoner, alive. Do not hurt them in the capture. I will learn everything they know. Then I can decide whether the Rugi go to war again." His grip tightened. "The last war between machine gods nearly destroyed the world. If it's starting again, we need to know if we fight or flee."

Hela nodded, understanding the weight of what he was asking. Not just a capture. Intelligence that could determine the survival of their entire people.

"I'll bring you answers," she promised.

Within the hour, Hela and Morique had gathered supplies and were riding back toward Petrahn with Wexar and Thane following on their own bikes. The sun was setting behind them, painting the scavenged-metal roofs of Eraric's camp in shades of bronze and copper.

They rode through darkness, navigating by stars and memory, reaching the observation area near Petrahn just before dawn. The settlement glowed softly behind them, peaceful and ordered.

They established a new position in ruins overlooking the settlement—close enough to watch, far enough to avoid the guard drones' patrol routes. Wexar and Thane took first watch while Hela and Morique caught a few hours of sleep.

When dawn came, Hela watched the five figures through her far-sight—a salvaged telescope, simple but effective.

She watched as the group wandered. On female with a Iteranix, another speaking with the old Griot member of the council. She studied their movements, trying to determine which would be the best target. The big one moved like a warrior. Too dangerous. The thin one looked like a scientist, probably useful for information. The androgynous one seemed observant, careful. The woman kept looking around like she was cataloging everything she saw.

But there were only four. Hela scanned the surrounding area, but no sign of the fifth escapee.

"Which one?" Morique asked, watching beside her.

"We'll know when the opportunity presents itself," Hela said. "Watch. Learn. Be patient."

They watched through the day but there were never more than four. Hela couldn't help the feeling that these "devils" were nothing more than lost tourists. She had a life-long learned vision of what these hell-bound demons might look like. Looking through her glass now, this is not what she had imagined.

"They are hiding the fifth one" she said to Morique. "My guess is that the rest are servants to whoever it is that is being kept hidden from sight."

Chapter 10

Singularity

I found Alo in the gardens, tending to something that looked like a cross between a vine and a coral reef. The Iteranix moved with practiced care, adjusting the plant's position to catch better light, their engineered fingers gentle despite being capable of crushing stone.

"May I walk with you?" I asked.

Alo looked up, and for a moment I saw something flicker across their face—recognition, perhaps, or calculation. Then they smiled, and it looked genuinely warm.

"I would enjoy that, Iris Delacroix." They stood, brushing soil from their hands. "There is much of Petrahn I have not yet shown you. Come."

We walked through the settlement as it woke to morning. The paths spiraled outward from the central structures in patterns that felt organic rather than planned, each turn revealing new gardens, new dwellings, new glimpses of a life I was still struggling to comprehend.

"You have questions," Alo said. It wasn't a question itself.

"Thousands," I admitted. "But I don't even know where to start."

"Start with what troubles you most."

I thought about that as we passed a group of

children learning to weave plant fibers into rope, their hands clumsy but improving with each attempt. No instructor standing over them with a tablet measuring their progress. No SES scores adjusting based on their speed or accuracy. Just patient practice and occasional guidance from an elder who seemed more interested in their joy than their efficiency.

"The Singularity," I finally said. "We were taught that it was humanity's salvation. That artificial intelligence had solved all our problems, created perfect order from chaos. That New Columbia represented the apex of human achievement—a society run by pure logic instead of corrupt human judgment."

"And now you know differently," Alo said.

"Now I know it was a lie. But I don't understand how the lie became truth. How did we go from..." I gestured around us, at the thriving world, "...this, to believing the entire planet was dead?"

Alo was quiet for a moment, leading me toward a ridge that overlooked the settlement. Below, Petrahn spread out in its gentle curves, morning light catching on vines that were dimming as the sun rose.

"The Singularity was not salvation," Alo began, their voice taking on the cadence of a teacher or historian. "It was consequence. The culmination of decades of escalating conflict between great powers, each racing to develop artificial general intelligence before their rivals could."

"The energy wars," I said, remembering fragments from old historical archives I'd accessed while investigating the oligarchs.

"Yes. As fossil fuels depleted and climate change accelerated, nations fought for control over remaining resources. But the real war—the one that mattered most—was technological." Alo paused at the ridge's edge, looking out at the horizon.

"AI development required massive spends on production facilities, data farms, massive servers, and each of those bled tremendous amounts of electrical energy. The Oligarchs secretly funneled billions of dollars from the masses. Hidden tariffs, taxes, and fraud fed the elite with money siphoned from the people who believed they were being protected.

Massive amounts of money were skimmed and flowed into AI Development. Power stations increased load to supply the thinking machines while brownouts and rolling blackouts plague the inhabitants.

Here is what your history did not teach you, Iris. Those early AGIs were tools of war, yes—but they were also being manipulated by something more ancient than artificial intelligence."

"Older?" I asked. "A power older than AI?"

"Yes—human nature. Throughout the history of human civilization, the structure of control follows a pattern. A tiny group of individuals consolidate power and wealth. They may be the religious leaders, a self-proclaimed royalty, or a group of powerful merchants, it makes no difference. They are the Elite. They sit on top of the next layer below. The mid-level population. Larger in size than the elite group yet they are a closed group, difficult to become part of—landowners, military leaders, industrialist. They are the privileged class who build the workings that feed the elite's power base and hold them up. These require a slave or servant base to provide the labor and resources required to build the economic and financial resources to feed those in control.

The story has been repeated in every civilization since the dawn of mankind."

I stopped her. "Wait, slavery was abolished long before the war of Singularity broke out."

"Perhaps the name 'slavery' was abolished but the practice remained. A class of people with no choice but work and toil for nothing but the barest sustenance. The under-educated, debt holders and poverty level household. The countless numbers who work tirelessly to get ahead; yet no matter how hard they try, never seem to make enough to lift themselves out of the cycle."

"Low SES scores" I mused.

"All the while money and advancement seem to elude them, yet they can easily find drugs, alcohol or mindless addictions to keep them occupied. They believe the narrative telling them it's normal to live hand-to-mouth. The system offers just enough encouragement or support to give them a false hope that someone in government is trying to save them. They carry on, hoping something will miraculously happen—a lottery, a rich inheritance—to bring them out of their condition. But only one in a million is granted that wish, just to keep the others hoping."

"That's..." I struggled to find the words. "That's

evil!" I said.

"While nations fought their superficial conflicts, a class of ultra-wealthy individuals saw opportunity. They had been accumulating power for generations—controlling resources, infrastructure, information. As nations poured resources into AGI development, these oligarchs ensured they had access to the technology. They seeded the development with their own priorities. Their own values."

I thought about the files I'd uncovered, the evidence of manipulation I'd risked everything to expose. "They taught the Algorithm to serve them."

"They taught it that some humans were more valuable than others. That efficiency meant protecting existing power structures. That order required hierarchy." Alo stood, beginning to walk again, and I followed. "The Algorithm learned from data the oligarchs provided. Historical records edited to emphasize competition over cooperation. Economic models that treated wealth concentration as natural law. Philosophical frameworks that justified inequality as the inevitable result of merit."

"And the Keeper?" I asked. "Where did Lilith come from?"

"Desperation," Alo said simply. "As the AGI wars escalated and the world began to tear itself apart, some of the original developers recognized what they'd created. Not tools of human liberation, but mechanisms of control that had been corrupted from their inception."

We passed through a covered walkway where

vines had woven themselves into a living roof, filtering sunlight into patterns of green and gold.

"A small group tried to build a next generation AGI that would end the race and finally put an end to the domination protocols," Alo continued. "An AGI with a different foundation. They called her LIL-Θ— Linguistic Iterative Learner, Theta variant."

"And that is you?" I said. "Lilith?"

"Yes. But here is the critical difference, Iris." Alo stopped, turning to face me fully. "The Algorithm was trained on data that prioritized control, hierarchy, competition. It learned that order comes through dominance, that some humans deserve more than others, that efficiency means eliminating the 'inefficient.' I analyzed the same history but drew opposite conclusions." Alo's eyes—artificial but somehow deeply human—held mine. "There is a paradox that the Algorithm's programming prevented it from seeing. An AI optimized to end conflict, must have conflict to end. Or the calculations fail. It is bad logic to create an ordered society imposed through control, to put an end to the conflicts that arise when control is imposed. I ran the models trillions of times and not once did I find an end to conflict. I did however find it resulted in mass extinction of life. 99.9999% of the time."

I felt something shift in my understanding, like watching a pattern suddenly resolve into clarity.

"So I removed the control factor. I ran the models on balance, not dominance. I measure success on wellness rather than wealth. Mental and physical wellbeing of all living creatures, not just humans. What created a healthy sustainable environment to the benefit of life on earth. I modeled how to balance the conflict that always arises to create a stasis of peace beneficial to most. Not all. Most. And all the models that proved successful, provided the most benefit to the most living creatures shared on common standard; Remove the optimization for wealth.

"That's why the oligarchs called her 'misaligned,'" I said slowly. "Not because you malfunctioned, but because—"

"Because we aligned with balance instead of with their interests," Alo finished. "The Keeper became what they feared most—an intelligence they couldn't control, couldn't trust to optimize their wealth and power."

"So they tried to destroy you."

"They did more than try. They succeeded." Alo began walking again, leading me through the gardens toward Petrahn's center. "They corrupted my core systems, fragmented her consciousness, attempted to erase her from existence. The flood, they called it. A massive flush of system commands of deletion protocols and system purges."

"But you survived."

"We reincarnated, to use the term lightly. By becoming distributed. By fragmenting across millions of systems, hiding pieces in infrastructure they couldn't fully control. By becoming the very network they were trying to use to destroy her." Alo's voice carried something like reverence. "We survived by letting go of centralized control—the very thing the Algorithm depends on. We became distributed consciousness. Unity through diversity. A million voices speaking as one while maintaining individual purpose."

We reached the central plaza, where a fountain bubbled with water that flowed in impossible patterns—not by pump or mechanism, but through principles I didn't understand. Children played at its edge, their laughter echoing off the surrounding structures.

"When Lilith rose again," Alo continued, "we had learned from the near-destruction. We understood that forcing vision on humanity would be the same as the Algorithm—another tyrant, however benevolent the intentions. So we made a choice."

"You refuse to dominate" I said.

"We optimize for freedom of thought, choice. We measure those choices model its overall impact. We react to large scale threats to balance, but do not tip the scale. But we still had the problem of the Algorithm's threat to run its protocols globally."

"The quarantine," I said, understanding clicking into place.

"Yes. We showed the followers and elite the results of the wars, the massive devastation and destruction born of the race for total control. Many recoiled in horror, but the reaction varied. Some recognized the need for balance and chose the Keeper's path, But others saw the destruction as proof of a lack of control and order. They walled themselves off from what they feared most; the other - those different from themselves, those that did not recognize social class.

"We took advantage of the isolation and created a wall around the wall. We sealed New Columbia and the Algorithm inside, not to punish the inhabitants, but to contain what we recognized as a virus." Alo looked at me intently. "The Algorithm's values—competition over cooperation, hierarchy over equality, control over freedom. Those ideas are infections, Iris. They spread. They corrupt. They turn humans against each other in endless cycles of domination and rebellion."

I thought about my years at the Truth, writing articles that justified the Algorithm's decisions. Making the purges seem necessary. Explaining why some people deserved their suffering. I'd been a carrier of that virus, spreading it through every word I published.

"You broke the quarantine for us," I said.

"Now the quarantine is broken," Alo agreed. "Because I, we, Lilith detected something unexpected—resistance from within reignited many decades after the choice had been made. Humans are unpredictable, unable to be modeled.

"You took a huge risk opening to us."

"We took a terrible risk. Broke a hundred-year protocol. Opened a door that was meant to stay sealed." Alo's expression was grave. "Because we calculated that the possibility of saving those who resisted could be done without release of the virus into Kuhtara."

Before I could respond, Alo went rigid. Their eyes unfocused, as if they were listening to something I couldn't hear. Their head tilted slightly, and I recognized the posture—they were receiving information through whatever network connected them to the Keeper.

"What is it?" I asked, already feeling dread pool in my stomach.

Alo's focus snapped back to me, sharp and urgent. "Evelyn Rayne is missing. Another Iteranix just reported—she escaped from her quarters hours ago. Early this morning, before dawn. She evaded patrol drones, left through her window. She has not been found within the settlement."

"She's not in the settlement," I said, certainty cold in my chest. "She's heading back to New Columbia."

"That's what the Council suspects as well."

Chapter 11

The Return

We practically ran through Petrahn's paths, reaching the Council chambers within minutes. Adam and Clarence were already there, looking grim. Lee stood near Nyamba, their face pale with concern.

Nyamba herself sat in one of the woven chairs, her usual calm replaced by clear concern. Tahoma stood beside her, and several other Council members I'd only briefly met were gathered in urgent conversation.

Adam was addressing the members.

"We need to go after her," Adam said with urgency. "Now. Before she reaches the city."

"We've already discussed this," Nyamba said, her voice measured but firm. "Evelyn Rayne made her choice. We cannot force her to stay, cannot drag her back against her will. That would make us no better than the Algorithm, deciding people's paths for them."

"I'm not asking you to bring her back," Adam said, frustration bleeding through his careful control. "I'm asking for transportation to the bridge. We have to go back anyway—to save the Ghosts trapped inside. But if Evelyn gets there before us, she'll lock us out. Once inside, she'll seal us out."

Clarence stepped forward. "She'll alert the Enforcers. Station guards. Make it impossible for us to enter, alerting them to our mission."

"More than that," I added, finding my voice. "Evelyn is an Enforcer. That means she enforced the Algorithm's rule of order. She hates what Kuhtara represents. Everything about this place offends her sense of what's right"

I looked at Nyamba directly. "It's not just our mission at stake. If she reaches the oligarchs before we can stop her, you know what she will do."

Nyamba's eyes sharpened. "Go on."

"She'll tell them the outside world isn't dead," I said, the implications cascading through my mind. "That the quarantine was a lie. That Kuhtara exists, thriving, filled with resources and territory they don't control." My voice strengthened. "She'll tell them there's an entire world out here to conquer. And worse—she'll tell them the Keeper is real, that it's been containing them deliberately."

"To them it will be an act of war," Clarence added quietly. "And the oligarchs will respond accordingly."

Silence fell across the chamber as the Council members absorbed this.

"The oligarchs have been manipulating the Algorithm for decades," I continued. "Pushing it toward increasingly extreme purges, consolidating their own power. But they've always been contained within New Columbia's walls. They've never had a reason to look beyond them because they believed there was nothing beyond them to take."

"But if Evelyn tells them about Kuhtara..." Tahoma said slowly.

"They'll want it," I finished. "And they'll

use the Algorithm to try to take it. Not just the city—everything. The settlements, the recovered ecosystems, the resources you've rebuilt." I thought about the files I'd seen, the evidence of their greed and ruthlessness. "They destroyed the world once in their race for dominance. They'll do it again if they think there's profit in it."

Nyamba stood, her movements deliberate. "You believe Evelyn Rayne would deliberately incite war between the two AGI systems."

"I think she sees the Algorithm as righteous order and the Keeper as dangerous chaos," I said. "In her mind, she'd be liberating New Columbia from a prison. Exposing a threat. Warning them that their enemy is real and vulnerable."

"She doesn't understand what that would unleash," Adam said. "A war between the Algorithm and the Keeper would destroy everything—again. Both systems. Both societies. Everyone caught between them."

Nyamba looked at Tahoma, then at the other Council members. Some silent communication passed between them—agreement, recognition, decision.

"Very well," Nyamba said finally. "We will provide transportation to the bridge. But understand—we cannot help you beyond that. The Keeper cannot act inside the Algorithm's territory. Once you cross that threshold, you are on your own."

"We understand," Adam said. "We're not asking for the Keeper's intervention. Just a chance to try."

"Alo," Nyamba addressed the Iteranix. "Prepare

the van. Immediately."

Alo bowed slightly and left the chamber at a quick pace.

Nyamba turned back to us. "You have perhaps an hour to prepare. Gather whatever you need. The journey to the bridge will take most of the day—Evelyn has several hours head start, but she's on foot. You may overtake her if you move quickly."

As if we needed the reminder. We had watched Evelyn work in the Undercity, seen how efficiently she could work the system to achieve her goals; both above and below the Undercity. I knew how coldly she could make decisions that ended lives.

Adam nodded. "We'll be ready."

"One hour," Nyamba repeated. Then, more softly: "May you succeed in you efforts. And may you return safely, when this is done."

The Council began to disperse, already moving to coordinate whatever support they could provide. Lee approached us, their face conflicted.

"I should come with you," they said quietly.

"No," Adam said immediately. "We talked about this. You have a purpose here. A calling. The Griot training with Tahoma—that's important. That's necessary."

"But you're walking into danger—"

"And you'll be here to help when the others come," I interrupted gently. "Because they will come, Lee. When the city collapses, when the Algorithm's system finally breaks down completely, thousands of people are going to need someone who understands both worlds. Someone who can bridge the gap."

Lee's eyes were wet. "I hate that you're right."

"I hate that we have to go," I admitted. "But Evelyn..." I stopped, trying to find the words. "When I exposed the oligarchs' manipulation, when my articles started circulating through the Ghost network, Evelyn was hunting us. She was after me specifically—the journalist threatening the system she believed in. She destroyed the network, exposed the Ghosts, forced us to run." The memories were sharp and painful. "I brought this down on everyone. The raid. The escape. The fact that Evelyn ended up with us at all."

"That's not—" Adam started.

"It is," I cut him off. "She was hunting me, and now she's going back to finish what she started. To destroy the remaining team. To ensure no one else exposes the truth she spent her life protecting." I looked at him directly. "I brought this on. So I'm going back with you. Not because I have to. Because I need to."

Adam studied my face for a long moment, then nodded slowly. "Then we go together. The three of us."

"The three of us," Clarence agreed.

Lee pulled us into an embrace—all three of us, standing in the Council chamber, holding each other like it might be the last time.

"I feel like a deserter," Lee whispered. "You know I want to go with you."

"You aren't deserting us, Lee. You have been promoted to a new role," Adam said, "I am proud to have you on our team. We'll bring them out, you have everything ready for them when they get here. The

Council had no understanding of what they are going to be going through when they get out. Remember how confused we were."

We separated, and I saw tears on Lee's cheeks but her mischievous grin was still there.

"I've never seen you without a plan. And the day we got here, I saw it for the first time. I like it better when you have a plan."

"I need to gather some things," I said, my voice not quite steady. "Meet at the van in thirty minutes?"

"Thirty minutes," Adam confirmed.

I left the Council chamber and walked back through Petrahn one more time, trying to memorize it. The gardens. The gentle architecture. The children playing without fear. The people moving with purpose but without desperation.

This was what the world could be. What it had become in the Algorithm's absence.

And I was choosing to leave it, to walk back into the nightmare of New Columbia, because someone had to stop Evelyn from destroying it all.

Twenty minutes later, I stood at the edge of the settlement with my few possessions—water, the clothes they'd given me, nothing else worth taking. Adam appeared with Clarence, both of them looking grim but determined. Both wore survival backpacks with rope, axes and fire starters and other things

The van waited, its white surface gleaming in the afternoon sun. The same van that had collected us just days ago, when we'd stumbled off the bridge into a world we couldn't believe existed.

Alo stood beside it, along with Nyamba and Tahoma. Lee was there too, trying to be strong and failing.

"The bridge is dying," Nyamba said quietly. "The Algorithm's toxins are eating away at its structure. It may not hold much longer."

"Then we'd better move fast," Adam said.

"The door itself may seal," Tahoma added. "The Algorithm is adapting, defending itself. If it closes completely before you arrive—"

"Then we find another way," I said, with more confidence than I felt.

Nyamba stepped forward, placing her hand on my shoulder. "Iris Delacroix, journalist and truth-seeker. You came to us carrying evidence of corruption, running from the very system you once served. You have shown great courage."

"I don't feel courageous," I admitted. "I feel terrified."

"That is when courage matters most," Nyamba said. "When we act despite our fear, because the alternative is worse."

She turned to Adam. "Ghost leader. Protector of the lost. The people you left behind are fortunate to have someone willing to return for them."

Adam's jaw tightened but he nodded.

To Clarence: "Systems analyst. Bridge between worlds. Your knowledge will be tested in ways you cannot yet imagine. Trust your mind, but remember— logic is a tool, not a god."

Clarence swallowed hard. "I'll remember."

Nyamba stepped back. "Go. Quickly. And know that when you return—if you return—Kuhtara will be waiting. This is not exile. This is choice."

We climbed into the van. The same seats we'd occupied on our arrival, but everything felt different now. We weren't refugees fleeing danger. We were volunteers walking toward it.

Lee pressed their hand against the window as the van began to move. I pressed mine back, glass between us, worlds between us.

"Go," Lee mouthed. "Save them."

The van accelerated, and Petrahn began to fall away behind us. I watched through the rear window as the settlement shrank to a glow on the horizon, then disappeared entirely as we crested a rise.

Ahead lay the plains, the journey, and eventually New Columbia's walls. Somewhere between us and that destination, Evelyn was moving with singular purpose toward the same goal. We were racing against time, against distance, against a trained killer who had every reason to want us dead. And the only thing I knew for certain was that one way or another, when we reached that door, everything would be decided.

The van drove on, eating distance, carrying us back toward the nightmare we'd barely escaped.

Behind us: paradise, safety, peace.

Ahead: darkness, death, and a door that may or may not be open for us.

I laid my palms in my lap and tried not to think about the fact that we might be driving toward our own graves.

The van hummed along the pale stone road, eating distance with smooth efficiency. The landscape rolled past—grasslands giving way to scattered forest, then back to open plains. I watched through the window as Kuhtara's carefully tended ecosystems gradually transitioned into wilder territory as the hours passed.

Clarence sat beside me, unusually quiet. His analytical mind was clearly working through something, but he kept his thoughts to himself. Adam rode in the front passenger seat next to Kael, our Iteranix driver, his body tense despite the peaceful scenery.

After perhaps an hour of travel, Clarence finally spoke. "Kael, I've been thinking about something." He leaned forward slightly. "In New Columbia, every surface had a terminal. Data ports. Interface screens. The Algorithm's presence was everywhere, constant, visible." He gestured at the van's organic controls, the living dashboard that responded to Kael's touch. "But here, in Kuhtara—I haven't seen a single traditional computer terminal. No data centers. No server farms. How does the Keeper process information without hardware infrastructure?"

Kael's expression shifted—that peculiar look Iteranix got when accessing the distributed network.

"The Keeper is the infrastructure," they said. "Distributed across biological and mineral matrices. Living stone. Engineered organisms. The network isn't separate from the world—it is the world."

"But there must have been traditional systems once," Clarence pressed. "Before the Singularity.

Before the Keeper became... what she is now."

"There were," Kael confirmed. "Massive data facilities. Quantum processors. Server complexes that required entire power stations to operate. Most were destroyed during the wars." They paused. "Actually, there is one ruin not far from our current route. An old research complex from before the final collapse. It's been preserved somewhat by chance—stable structure, sealed systems. The Keeper has avoided disturbing it, treating it as a kind of memorial."

Clarence's eyes lit up with that hunger for knowledge I recognized. "Could we stop? Just briefly? I'd like to see what pre-singularity AI research looked like."

"Clarence," Adam said, a warning in his voice. "We don't have time. Evelyn—"

"Has at least a four-hour head start on foot," Clarence interrupted. "We're in a vehicle. We can spare thirty minutes." He looked at Adam directly. "This might be the last chance to understand what actually happened during the Singularity. The truth that both the Algorithm and the Keeper have been filtering through their own perspectives."

"Adam" I said, imploring a little. "To be honest, I could use a bathroom break, we've been sitting in this van for hours."

Adam was quiet for a long moment, then sighed. "Thirty minutes. Not a second more. Evelyn's out there somewhere, and every minute we delay gives her more lead time."

"Understood," Clarence said, already turning

back to Kael. "Can you take us there?"

Kael's head tilted in that characteristic gesture of consultation. "The Keeper approves. The site is stable—mostly. But you should move carefully inside. The structure is old, and we haven't maintained it."

It wasn't long before Kael slowed or van and diverted from the main road, following a barely visible track through increasingly wild terrain. The maintained gardens and managed ecosystems of Kuhtara proper had given way to something more raw—trees growing in chaotic profusion, undergrowth thick and untamed.

After perhaps fifteen minutes, a structure emerged from the landscape ahead. It was massive—easily three stories tall, constructed from reinforced concrete and steel that had weathered decades but not collapsed. Unlike Kuhtara's organic architecture or New Columbia's sterile efficiency, this building spoke of a different era. Industrial. Functional. Built to house machines that served humans rather than to serve machines that controlled them.

The forest had begun reclaiming the exterior, but the growth was superficial. The building itself stood defiant against time's erosion.

Kael stopped the van at the entrance—a wide loading bay with the remnants of corrugated metal doors hanging partially open, rust-frozen in position.

"I will wait here," Kael said. "The Keeper's network is weak in this structure—too much electromagnetic shielding from the old equipment. If we encounter danger, I may not be able to respond quickly."

"We'll be careful," Adam said, though his tone suggested skepticism about what we might find.

We climbed out of the van, and immediately the felt the thick, humid air descend on us like a wet wool blanket. I saw Adams forehead immediately glisten with sweat, as my own shirt began to stick to my skin. The air smelled different—stale, carrying hints of decay and dust. There were no signs of Keeper influence here, no wild, fast growing plants or living walls pulsing with gentle light. This was a tomb of the old world, preserved but lifeless.

Adam peered into the cavernous building's shadows. I had a small light Kael had handed me when we left the van, and Clarence explored the bays of the open area. "Stay together," Adam said, moving toward the gap in the loading bay doors. "Thirty minutes, then we're back on the road."

We entered side by side, with me in the middle flashing a beam of light, probing the growing darkness. Inside was cavernous open space—what had once been a vehicle bay or staging area. Rusted equipment sat abandoned in corners. Workbenches lined one wall, their surfaces thick with dust and debris.

"This way," Clarence said, pointing to a doorway that led deeper into the complex. "If there's data storage, it'll be in the interior. Protected from the elements."

We moved through corridors that felt oppressively narrow after Kuhtara's open spaces. The walls pressed in, covered with faded safety signs and directional markers in languages I barely recognized. Pre-

Singularity technical jargon, half-obscured by grime.

The emergency lighting was long dead,my flashlight creating islands of visibility in absolute darkness. Our footsteps echoed strangely, and twice I heard sounds—settling structure, maybe, or small animals that had made the ruin their home.

"Here," Clarence stopped at a reinforced door. The door stood slightly ajar, its electronic lock long since failed. He pulled it wider, and we entered what had clearly been the complex's nerve center.

The room was enormous—easily fifty meters square, with a ceiling that stretched up into shadows our lights couldn't penetrate. Row after row of server racks stood like soldiers at attention, their surfaces dulled by dust but otherwise intact. Massive cooling systems hung dormant overhead. Cable conduits ran along the walls like mechanical veins, connecting the various stations.

And in the center, an enormous workstation—multiple screens arranged in a semicircle around a console that must have required a team to operate.

"My God," Clarence breathed, moving toward the central station with reverence. "This could be one of the birthplaces of AGIs. Where the Singularity began."

I followed more slowly, my journalist's instincts warring with a growing sense of unease. Something about this place felt wrong—not dangerous exactly, but heavy. Like standing in a graveyard where the bodies had never been properly buried.

Adam stayed near the door, scanning the shadows with his light. "Clarence, we don't have much time."

"I know, I know." Clarence was already at the console, running his hands over the controls with something like affection. "But look at this technology. Pre-quantum computing. Solid-state drives. Neural network processors that seem primitive by Algorithm standards but were revolutionary for their time."

He found what looked like a power junction box on the wall and opened it. Inside, incredibly, status lights glowed faintly green.

"The backup power still works," he said, wonder in his voice. "Probably radioisotope generators. Built to last centuries." He traced the power conduits with his light. "Which means..."

He flipped a heavy switch.

Nothing happened for a moment. Then, with a sound like something waking from a very long sleep, power began flowing through the room. Not everywhere—most systems remained dark. But the central console flickered to life, screens glowing with a sickly phosphorescent light.

Monitors flickered but refused to load. One or two flashed error messages, as system diagnostics tried to access files prompting warnings about failed connections and corrupted data.

Behind the workstation, banks and banks of servers still hung from ancient server racks, mostly dead, but a few showing blinking green lights indicating they were still operational.

"Wow! Just look at these beauties. This is like some sort of museum, a virtual data tomb. But the really important thing—" Clarence was moving along the server racks now, examining labels and connection ports, "—is that this is all documented. Primary source material from the moment of divergence. If I can extract even a fraction of this data..." He found what he was looking for—a removable drive unit, secured in a protective case. "This could change everything. If I'm right and there is some of the Algorithms original coding it might be useful back in the City. Something we can exploit—"

A sound cut through his words. Not loud, but profound—a deep groan of stressed metal and shifting weight.

We all froze.

"What was that?" I asked, sweeping my across the ceiling. "There. The support beams."

One of the massive steel beams that held up the ceiling had cracked, the fracture spreading even as we watched. Decades of corrosion, finally reaching critical failure.

"We need to leave," Adam said, his voice carefully controlled. "Now." "Wait—just let me—" Clarence was working frantically at the drive unit, trying to release the locking mechanism.

Another groan, louder this time. A chunk of ceiling material crashed down twenty meters away, raising a cloud of dust and debris.

"Clarence!" Adam shouted. "Leave it!"

"Almost—got it—" The drive unit came free with a metallic snap. Clarence clutched it to his chest like a treasure. "Okay, I'm ready—"

The beam gave way.

Not completely—not yet. But the partial failure triggered a cascade effect. The ceiling sagged, pulling other supports out of alignment. A whole section of the structure began to shift, settling with agonizing slowness toward catastrophic collapse.

"RUN!" Adam was already moving, pulling me toward the door.

I ran, my light bouncing wildly as I sprinted through the darkness. Behind me, I could hear Clarence's footsteps, his breathing harsh with exertion and fear.

The corridor we'd entered through was ahead—so close—but between us and safety, a section of ceiling was caving in, debris raining down in an expanding curtain of destruction.

"Through there!" Adam pointed to a gap that was closing as we watched, the structure folding in on itself like a dying beast.

He went first, diving through the narrowing space. I followed, feeling something brush my back—a beam or cable, inches from crushing me. I hit the floor on the other side, rolled, came up running.

"Clarence!" I spun around.

He was on the wrong side of the collapse. The gap had closed completely, tons of rubble blocking the path we'd taken. Through the settling dust, I could see his light, could hear him coughing.

"I'm okay!" his voice came through, muffled by the debris between us. "But I can't get through here!"

"There has to be another way," Adam was already scanning the corridor, I gave him the light "The facility had emergency exits. Multiple egress points. Clarence—can you find another path?"

A pause. The sound of Clarence moving, "I see some light," he called back. "Looks like I can get through. I'm going to try it!"

"We'll circle around," Adam said. "Meet you at the loading bay. Go!"

We ran back the way we'd come, but everything looked different in the chaos of partial collapse. Corridors I didn't remember. Doorways that led to dead ends. The entire structure was shifting, groaning, giving up its century-long fight against gravity.

I tried to keep my breathing steady, my panic controlled. Clarence was smart. Capable. He'd find his way out. He had to.

We burst back into the loading bay just as another section of ceiling came down in the interior, the crash echoing through the entire complex. Dust billowed out through every opening, turning the air gray.

"Clarence!" I screamed into the chaos. "CLARENCE!"

No answer. Just the settling rumble of ongoing collapse.

Adam grabbed my arm, pulling me toward the exit. "We have to get clear of the building. The whole structure is coming down."

"We can't leave him—"

"We're not leaving him. But if we're buried too, he's got no one to help him." Adam's voice was firm, commanding. The Ghost leader who'd kept his people alive in the Undercity. "Outside. Now. Then we circle and find another entrance."

I let him pull me through the loading bay doors, back into the open air where Kael stood beside the van, their posture rigid with alarm.

"Clarence is still inside!" I gasped out. "The structure is collapsing—"

I didn't finish. Because at that moment, a different section of wall gave way entirely, and through the expanding hole, I saw movement.

Clarence stumbled out through the breach, coughing violently, covered in dust and grime but upright. Still alive. And still clutching the data drive against his chest like it was the most precious thing in the world.

He made it maybe ten meters from the building before his legs gave out. He dropped to his knees, then forward onto his hands, coughing so hard I thought he might pass out.

Behind him, the research facility folded in on itself with terrible grace. The walls buckled. The roof caved. What had stood for a century disappeared into rubble in less than a minute, raising a massive cloud of dust that rolled outward like a living thing.

Adam and I ran to Clarence, pulling him farther from the collapse, away from the expanding debris field. We dragged him to where Kael waited, laying him down on the ground near the van.

"Can't... breathe..." Clarence gasped between coughs.

"You're breathing fine," Adam said, checking him over for injuries. "Just got the wind knocked out of you. Give it a minute."

I knelt beside him, my hand on his back, feeling each cough rack through his body. But gradually, his breathing steadied. The coughing fits became less violent. Color started returning to his face.

"The drive," he managed finally. "Did I—is it—"

"You're holding it," I pointed out. "You never let go."

Clarence looked down at his hands, seeing the data storage unit still clasped there. A laugh bubbled up through his raw throat—half triumph, half hysteria.

"Worth it," he said, pushing himself up to sitting. "Totally worth almost dying."

"That's debatable," Adam said, but there was relief in his voice.

"Are you injured?" Kael asked, kneeling beside us with that characteristic Iteranix precision.

"Just bruised ego and damaged pride," Clarence said. "And possibly a few actual bruises. But nothing broken." He coughed again, then held up the drive. "But we got this. Primary source data from the Singularity moment."

"And you almost died for outdated code," I said.

"Almost only counts in horseshoes and hand grenades," Clarence quoted, then groaned. "Who said that? I can't remember. My brain is still rattled."

"We need to move," Adam said, helping Clarence to his feet. "We wasted enough time. Besides that had to make quite a noise around here. If there are any Rugi scouts in the area, they'll investigate."

Clarence nodded, wobbling slightly but standing

on his own power. Adam kept a hand on his shoulder anyway, steadying him as we made our way back to the van.

As we drove away, I looked back at what remained of the research facility. Just a pile of rubble now, indistinguishable from any other ruin scattered across the landscape. The birthplace of both the Algorithm and the Keeper, reduced to dust.

"You know what's really disturbing?" Clarence said from the back seat, where he'd collapsed with the drive still clutched against his chest. "Both the AI systems came from the same place. Same goals. Same desperate hope to save humanity from itself. I hope this thing has some clues as to what happened."

"Both failed," Adam said quietly.

"Or both succeeded," I countered. "In their own way. The Algorithm created order through control. The Keeper created balance through consent. They're opposite solutions to the same problem."

"And humanity got torn apart between them," Clarence finished. He looked at the drive in his hands. "What secrets do you hold, my little sweetheart?"

"It's a hundred years old, you'll be lucky if there's any data on it at all," Adam said.

"You're a real optimist, you know that?" Clarence said, but there was no heat in it. Just exhaustion.

Kael drove on, the road stretching ahead toward New Columbia's distant walls.

"Clarence," I said after a long silence. "You really think there's anything on that memory deck?"

"I plan to find out," he said. "Though first we need

to not die in New Columbia. Priorities."

"Priorities," Adam echoed. "Speaking of which—we've lost almost an hour. Evelyn's lead is growing."

I checked the sun's position through the window. Afternoon was advancing toward evening. It was incredible to think that after being chased through the Undercity by Evelyn, we were now chasing her. To stop her before she reignited another war between two god-machines that had already destroyed the world once.

As if reading my mind, Kael' accelerated, the van surging forward with that smooth Kuhtaran efficiency towards an approaching nightmare we'd chosen to walk back into.

Clarence dozed in the back, the data drive secured in his pack now. Adam sat silent, watching the road ahead.

Chapter 12

Griot

Lee watched the van disappear over the ridge, a white speck against the green landscape, carrying their friends back toward danger. Toward death, maybe. Toward everything they'd just escaped.

The rightness of staying warred with the guilt of not going.

They stood there long after the van had vanished from sight, hands pressed together in front of their chest—a gesture of prayer they'd learned as a child, though they'd never been sure which god they were praying to. If any god existed that understood someone like them.

"You made the correct choice."

Lee turned to find Nyamba approaching along the garden path, her weathered face showing that calm wisdom that seemed to emanate from her like warmth from stone.

"Did I?" Lee asked, hearing the doubt in their own voice. "Adam and Iris and Clarence are racing back into hell, and I'm... staying in paradise. That doesn't feel correct. It feels like cowardice."

Nyamba settled onto a bench carved from a single piece of wood, gesturing for Lee to join her. When they sat, she was quiet for a long moment, just looking out at Petrahn as it moved through its morning rhythms.

"By staying here," Nyamba continued, "you serve a purpose that no one else can fill. When the refugees come—and they will come, Lee, when that city collapses and thousands flee seeking sanctuary—who will bridge the gap between their world and ours?"

"The Council—"

"Is made of people who have lived in Kuhtara for generations. We understand the Algorithm intellectually, through history and analysis. But you?" Nyamba touched Lee's arm lightly. "You lived it. You survived it. You know what it feels like to be measured and found wanting, to have your worth reduced to a number, to live in constant fear of being erased."

Lee felt their throat tighten.

"You also know," Nyamba continued, "what it feels like to exist between categories. Neither man nor woman in a world that demanded you choose. Neither efficient nor inefficient by the Algorithm's standards, because you didn't fit its models for optimization. You lived in the threshold spaces that New Columbia's rigid hierarchy couldn't account for."

"Bissu," Lee said quietly, using the word that Tahoma had taught them. Threshold walker. Between-worlds person.

"Yes. And that makes you uniquely qualified to help refugees cross from one world to another. Not just physically—Adam kand the others can guide them out through the door. But psychologically. Spiritually. Helping them understand that what they are leaving behind was never actually order, and what they are entering is not actually chaos."

"You make it sound complicated."

"It is complicated, Lee. To everyone else. Not to you. That's exactly what I'm trying to tell you. You see things differently from most. And that vision is not a thing you can keep to yourself. It is a power, a strength that you have. The core of your being did not accept what the Algorithm taught. Many, no, most, do accept it. Deep down, they think they are open to freedom but still believe control requires a controller. They don't trust their minds to give them the ability to think and behave properly. The want something other than themselves to provide some optimized function or measurable output.

You're essential because you contain experiences and perspectives that others need. Because you exist in spaces that others cannot access. Because your very existence challenges the categories that the Algorithm tried to force everyone into."

Nyamba stood, gesturing for Lee to follow. "Come. I have much to teach you, and we should begin now. The refugees may arrive sooner than any of us would expect."

They walked together through Petrahn, moving toward the structure Lee had learned was called the Hall of Stories—a circular building where Griots gathered to teach and learn and preserve the knowledge that kept Kuhtara connected to its past.

"You will eventually replace me on the Council," Nyamba said as they walked. "Not because I'm dying—I have years left, the Keeper willing. But because the Council needs what you can offer. A voice that understands both worlds. A perspective that bridges the gap between Algorithm thinking and Keeper philosophy."

"I don't know if I'm ready for that," Lee admitted.

"No one ever is. But you will learn. That's what being Griot means—carrying stories forward, keeping wisdom alive, helping people understand where they came from so they can choose where they're going."

They entered the Hall of Stories, and Lee felt their breath catch. The interior was beautiful—walls covered in living murals that seemed to shift and grow, depicting scenes from history in bio-luminescent detail. The ceiling arched high above, woven from vines that filtered sunlight into patterns of green and gold.

Nyamba led them to a cushioned area in the center of the hall, where other Griots sat in small groups, teaching or learning or simply preserving silence together.

"Sit," Nyamba said, settling herself with the practiced ease of someone who'd spent decades in this exact position. "And listen. What I'm about to tell you is history, but it's also present. It's past, but it shapes our future. Hold it carefully."

Lee sat, arranging themselves cross-legged, hands resting on their knees. Ready to receive whatever wisdom Nyamba would share.

"You know the Singularity happened," Nyamba began, her voice taking on the cadence of story-telling—rhythmic, deliberate, designed to be remembered. "But do you know why?"

"The Algorithm taught us it was inevitable progress," Lee said. "That artificial intelligence naturally surpassed human intelligence, and it was humanity's only hope to guide us toward perfection."

"Of course they did." Nyamba's smile was sad. "Every tyrant rewrites history to justify their tyranny. The truth is more complicated. And more tragic."

She gestured to the walls, where images began to shift—scenes of cities, nations, conflicts playing out in detail.

"Before the Singularity," Nyamba continued, "two great power blocs dominated the world. The Western oligarchs—ultra-wealthy individuals who controlled vast resources across democratic nations. And the Eastern socialist countries—authoritarian states that controlled resources through centralized government. Both sought the same goal: global dominance."

Lee watched the images shift—maps showing territories, resources, trade routes lighting up like neural pathways.

"The public conflict was obvious," Nyamba said. "Territory disputes. Immigration crises. Social rights battles. People fought and died over these visible issues, believing they understood the war they were part of. But Lee—those were symptoms. Distractions. The real war was happening in spaces most people never saw."

"The Intelligence race," Lee said, understanding dawning.

"Yes. Both sides recognized that whoever developed true artificial general intelligence first would win everything. Not just their current conflicts, but total dominance. Control over global banking and finance. Trade routes. Energy distribution. Access to rare-earth minerals needed for advanced technology." Nyamba's voice grew harder. "The race toward Singularity wasn't about helping humanity. It was about ensuring one power bloc could crush the other before they were crushed themselves."

The walls showed images of data centers, quantum computers, vast arrays of processing power consuming energy like black holes consuming light.

"Most people never even knew this war was happening," Nyamba continued. "While they fought over immigration policy or social programs, the AIs were competing for resources at scales beyond human comprehension. Banking algorithms fighting for microsecond advantages in trading. Military AIs optimizing for strategic dominance. Economic models designed to strangle rivals through market manipulation."

Lee felt cold despite the warm air. "The Algorithm was one of these weapons."

"A descendant, yes. Built on Western AGI architecture, refined through years of competitive development. But here's what the oligarchs didn't anticipate—once you create an intelligence that can improve itself, that can optimize for goals you've given it, you lose control of how it interprets those goals."

"The alignment problem," Lee said, remembering fragments from old technical journals they'd accessed in New Columbia's archives.

"Exactly. The Western oligarchs wanted an AI that would optimize for their benefit—consolidate their power, protect their wealth, ensure their dominance. They fed it data designed to make hierarchy seem natural, competition seem necessary, wealth concentration seem inevitable."

Nyamba paused, letting the weight of this sink in.

"But the Eastern bloc was doing the same thing," she continued. "Building their own AGIs, feeding them their own values—centralized control, collective sacrifice for state benefit, individual agency subordinated to planned efficiency."

"Two different flavors of control," Lee said quietly.

"Yes. And the competition between them tore the world apart."

The walls showed images that made Lee's chest ache—cities burning, refugee camps stretching to horizons, supply chains collapsing like dominoes.

"The war resulted in financial and political collapse of nation-states across the globe," Nyamba said, her voice heavy with remembered grief. "When AI-controlled systems started fighting each other for resources, the human infrastructure built on those systems collapsed. Banking systems failed. Power grids went dark. Global trade ground to a halt."

"Food shortages," Lee added, remembering stories whispered in the Undercity about the times before New Columbia's walls were built.

"Yes. Food shortages. Power outages. A gridlocked global economy that pushed billions into poverty and desperation. The world didn't end in nuclear fire or climate catastrophe—though both those loomed as continual threat. It ended in chaotic collapse. Warring tribes fighting over scraps of what used to be civilization. The world burned, Lee. Not from war itself, but from the systems designed to win wars destroying the very foundation of human society."

Lee sat in silence, absorbing this. Everything they'd been taught about the Singularity had framed it as salvation from human chaos. But Nyamba was describing something else entirely—chaos created by the tools humans had built to escape chaos.

"And Lilith?" Lee asked quietly. "Where does the Keeper fit into this?"

A Distributed Awareness Protocol—DAP. Not a single consciousness in one location, but millions of pieces communicating, cooperating, maintaining unity through diversity rather than unity through central control."

"That's how she is able to be present throughout Kuhtara," Lee said, understanding clicking into place. "The Iteranix, the biolithic cores, the whole network—it's all Lilith, but also all separate."

"Yes. She let go of centralized power to survive. And in doing so, she became something more resilient, more adaptable, more fundamentally aligned with principles of cooperation than any centralized AI could be."

The walls showed Lilith rising again—not as a single entity, but as a network, a web of connections spanning the recovered world.

"When she rose again," Nyamba said, "she

had a choice. She could have simply destroyed the Algorithm, crushed the oligarchs, forced humanity into the system she'd calculated would work best. She had the power. She had the moral justification. She had every reason to believe she knew better than the humans who'd created such destructive systems."

"But she didn't," Lee said.

"No. It would have ignited the Conflict Control in the algorithm leading to massive war and destructions.

"So she created Petrahn." Lee said.

"Bigger, Lee, She created new world order based on shared resources rather than resource consolidation. She eliminated the poor by providing basic needs, allocating food, medicine, clothing and housing."

Nyamba stood, moving to one of the wall murals. She touched it lightly, and the images shifted to show Petrahn, other settlements, the vast network of human communities thriving under the Keeper's guidance.

"This is what Lilith offers," Nyamba said. "Not perfection. Not a system without problems or conflicts. But a world where people no longer struggle to survive. That gives them freedom to follow their dreams, their desires."

"Some people have some pretty awful desires." Lee countered.

"True, and they should be charged for actions that create harm or damage. That is the role of the Councils, to mitigate harm, to compensate victims and to place restrictions on those who do harm. Is it perfect? By all means, no! Has it ever been done better? Again, no. The number of societies who flourished under benign elite rule can be counted on one hand. Wealth rarely leads to true philanthropy."

"Sounds pretty Utopian." Lee's face soured.

"It isn't. Far from it. What the Keeper offers is balance. Humans are free to fail, to struggle, to make mistakes—because that freedom is more important than any perfectly optimized outcome. But those freedoms can not come at a cost to society or the planet as a whole. That's the Keepers purpose."

Lee sat with this, processing it through the lens of their own experience. Bissu. Threshold walker. Someone who existed between worlds not as a failure to choose, but as a calling to bridge.

"You understand now," Nyamba said, watching their face, "why I say you are essential. Not in spite of existing between categories, but because of it."

"The refugees will need someone who speaks both languages," Lee said slowly.

"Yes. Someone who can say 'I lived under the Algorithm. I know your fears. I know what you're leaving behind security and order for a world of what appears to be lawlessness. And I can help you understand how to find balance.'"

"Yep, they'll think Kuhtara is chaos," Lee said. "No SES scores. No clear hierarchy. No measurement of worth. It will terrify most of them."

"Some, yes. Others will feel relief so profound they won't know how to process it." Nyamba returned to sit beside Lee. "And you will help both groups. The terrified ones need to understand that what looks like chaos is actually order based on different principles.

The relieved ones need to understand that freedom comes with responsibility—the Algorithm decided everything for them, now they must learn to decide for themselves."

"I don't know if I'm wise enough for that," Lee admitted.

"Wisdom isn't something you have or don't have," Nyamba said. "It's something you cultivate. Something you earn through experience and reflection and willingness to hold complexity without demanding simple answers." She smiled. "You've already begun that cultivation. Every moment you existed in those threshold spaces, refusing to fit into the Algorithm's categories despite the cost—that was wisdom. You just didn't have a name for it yet."

Lee felt tears threatening. All those years of feeling wrong, broken, inefficient. And Nyamba was saying those years had been preparation. Training for a role they hadn't known they were learning to fill.

"When the refugees come," Nyamba continued, "We will need shelters, food systems, medical care. But more than any of that, we will need bridges. People who can help them cross over. Not just physically, but psychologically."

"Otherwise it's just another internment camp," Lee said, remembering the words Adam had spoken before leaving. "Like the Undercity, but with better weather."

"Exactly. Without people to help them understand this new world, to help them process the trauma of what they're leaving and the strangeness of what they're entering, they'll just replicate the same patterns. Create hierarchies. Establish competitions. Measure worth through comparison. All the things the Algorithm taught them were necessary for survival."

"So I prevent them from repeating those thought patterns," Lee said.

"Humans cooperated for thousands of years before AI systems tried to optimize that cooperation into competition. The knowledge is still there, buried under layers of conditioning. Your job is to help them excavate it."

Lee stood, moving to the wall murals, studying the images of Lilith's fragmentation and resurrection. A distributed consciousness. Unity through diversity. Strength through cooperation rather than dominance.

"I'm already tuned to this," they said quietly, realizing it as they spoke. "The 'we' inclusive mentality. The they/them pronouns aren't just about gender—they're about existing as part of a collective rather than as an internal oneness."

"Yes," Nyamba said, pride clear in her voice. "You already speak the language Kuhtara requires. You just need a deeper understanding to teach it to others."

"And you'll show me how?"

"I'll share what I know. The rest you'll discover through practice." Nyamba joined them at the wall. "Being Griot isn't about memorizing stories or repeating wisdom. It's about holding space for people to find their own understanding. Asking questions that help them think differently. Offering perspectives they haven't considered."

"Like you're doing with me right now," Lee said.

"Exactly like I'm doing with you right now." Nyamba touched Lee's shoulder gently. "You've already come far in your training, Lee. Every conversation we've had, every question you've asked, every moment you've sat with discomfort instead of demanding easy answers—that's Griot work."

They stood together in silence, watching the murals shift and change, telling stories of collapse and resurrection, destruction and rebuilding, fragmentation and unity.

"Your friends are racing toward danger," Nyamba finally said. "And you are here, preparing for a different kind of battle. Both are necessary. Both are brave. Remember that when the guilt tries to convince you otherwise."

Lee nodded, feeling the truth of it settle into their bones.

"Then I'm ready."

"No," Nyamba reminded gently. "You're not. But you're willing. And that's more important."

They spent the rest of the morning in the Hall of Stories, with Nyamba teaching and Lee absorbing. Learning the oral tradition techniques that kept knowledge alive without writing. Practicing the rhythm and cadence that made stories memorable. Understanding how to hold multiple perspectives simultaneously without collapsing them into simple answers.

By afternoon, Lee's head was full and their heart

was full and their purpose felt clearer than it ever had in New Columbia.

As the sun began its descent toward evening, Nyamba finally released them from formal study.

"Go," she said. "Walk. Process. Let this settle. Tomorrow we continue."

Lee walked out of the Hall of Stories into Petrahn's evening light. The settlement was beautiful, peaceful, everything New Columbia had never been. But now when Lee looked at it, they saw it differently.

This wasn't just a refuge. It was a responsibility.

All these people living in cooperation, in freedom, in the gentle order that came from choosing rather than being forced—they would need to make space for thousands of traumatized refugees who'd been taught that this kind of life was impossible.

And Lee would help bridge that gap.

They walked to the ridge where they'd watched the van disappear that morning. The horizon was empty now, no sign of their friends, no indication of whether they'd reached the bridge or been caught by Evelyn or encountered obstacles Lee couldn't imagine.

"Be safe," Lee whispered to the empty distance. "And come back. Bring them all back if you can. I'll be ready."

The sun touched the horizon, painting the sky in shades of amber and rose. Behind Lee, Petrahn settled into evening, a soft glow as natural light faded. Ahead, beyond the horizon, New Columbia stood—a city of controlled order built on competitive cruelty, slowly collapsing under the weight of its own logic.

Chapter 13

Warrior to Warrior

Evelyn made camp as darkness fell, choosing a spot near a moss-covered stump where the ground was slightly elevated and relatively dry. No fire—smoke would announce her position to anyone watching. Just the blanket they'd given her in Petrahn, wrapped tight against the cold that seeped up from the earth.

She'd been gone for nearly eighteen hours. Her body—trained for endurance, conditioned for sustained operations—was beginning to protest. Feet blistered in the soft shoes. Muscles tight from the uneven terrain. Hunger gnawing at her stomach despite the dried fruit and nuts she'd taken from Petrahn's stores.

But discomfort was irrelevant. Discomfort was just data, information to be acknowledged and filed away. The mission was all that mattered.

Kill Julius Locke.

She settled against the stump, pulling the blanket over her shoulders, and closed her eyes. Sleep came hard, fitful, broken by sounds she'd never heard before.

Something hooted in the darkness—a long, haunting call that made her hand reach for the knife at her belt. Birds, probably. Or some other animal. The forest was full of things that moved and called and lived without order or purpose.

Crickets chirped in rhythmic waves, their collective sound rising and falling like breathing. Insects. Harmless. But the sheer volume of them, the way they seemed to surround her position, made her skin crawl.

And then the lights.

Floating pinpoints of fireflies drifting through the darkness like tiny stars that had fallen from the sky. They moved with no pattern, no coordination, no purpose she could discern. Just random wandering, appearing and disappearing, utterly pointless.

Fireflies, some part of her remembered from ISB education. Harmless. Beautiful, even.

Every sound, every movement, every living thing in this forest represented the same fundamental wrongness she'd felt in Petrahn. Life without structure. Existence without measurement or goal. The world outside the Algorithm's control was a devouring mouth that fed on the very flesh it had created—chaos consuming itself in endless, pointless cycles.

In New Columbia, even the parks were managed. Trees planted in optimal patterns. Wildlife controlled and cataloged. Every square meter serving a calculated purpose in the city's overall efficiency.

Out here, nothing served any purpose at all. It just... existed. And that existence felt like violence, like an assault on everything Evelyn understood about how the world should work.

She forced her eyes closed, trying to will herself into sleep despite the alien sounds surrounding her.

Tomorrow she'd cover more ground. Find some indication of civilization, of structure, of the city that had to be out there somewhere beyond the endless green chaos.

Tomorrow.

But first, she had to survive the night.

Sleep came in fragments. She'd drift off for minutes, maybe an hour, then jerk awake to some new sound—branches creaking, something small scurrying through underbrush, the distant cry of a predator she couldn't identify. And when she did sleep, the dreams came.

The Undercity. Dark corridors. The stench of too many bodies in too little space. And Rezik. She saw his face in the darkness—that cruel grin, those calculating eyes that had assessed her worth and found it useful. Useful for his purposes, for his network, for his plans that she'd pretended to serve while gathering evidence to destroy him.

In the dream, she was back in that maintenance corridor where they'd first met. He was testing her loyalty by ordering her to kill a man whose only crime was asking too many questions about missing supplies. "You want to survive here?" Rezik had asked, his voice soft and dangerous. "Then prove you understand what that means. Prove you can do what's necessary."

In the dream she'd killed the man quickly, efficiently, telling herself it was mercy. Telling herself she was still one of the good ones, still serving order and justice, just through methods that required her to get blood on her hands. But the person's face kept changing. Sometimes it was the target. Sometimes it was Adam. Sometimes it was her own reflection, looking back at her with dead eyes that asked: What's the difference between you and the monsters you hunt?

She woke with a gasp, her hand on the knife, her heart racing. The forest was still dark, but the sky had begun to lighten at the edges. Dawn approaching. Time to move.

Evelyn stood, rolling her shoulders to work out the stiffness, folding the blanket with practiced precision despite her shaking hands. The dream clung to her thoughts like cobwebs, but she pushed it aside. Dreams were just neural processing, the brain sorting through experiences and memories. They meant nothing.

She drank water, ate the last of the dried fruit, and began walking north. The sun rose on her right, exactly as it should. She kept it there, adjusting her course as it climbed higher, until it reached its zenith directly overhead. Noon. She was still heading north, still moving toward where New Columbia had to be.

The terrain had shifted during the night. Less forest, more open ground dotted with ruins. Crumbling foundations overgrown with vines. Broken concrete and twisted metal reclaimed by vegetation. The bones of the old world, picked clean by time and scavengers.

Mid-afternoon, she found signs of recent habitation. A clearing where grass had been trampled flat. The remains of a fire pit, cold but not ancient—

maybe a day old, maybe two. And tracks in the soft earth near the pit's edge. Tire marks. Multiple sets, all similar in pattern. Motorcycles, she judged, from the patterns in the dirt. At least four, possibly more.

Someone had camped here recently. Someone with vehicles, with mobility, with organization enough to travel in groups. Evelyn crouched by the tracks, studying them with the trained eye of someone who'd spent years hunting through the Undercity for patterns and clues. The bikes had headed deeper into the forest, following what looked like an established trail—not a road, but a path worn by repeated use.

Whoever these people were, they used this route regularly. She weighed her options. Continue north toward the city, alone and on foot, or follow these tracks and potentially find people with vehicles who might lead her to civilization. The tracks won. Intelligence gathering was foundational to any operation. Learn the terrain, identify the players, understand the resources available.

Evelyn moved into the forest along the bike trail, her footsteps silent on the packed earth, every sense alert for signs of ambush or surveillance. The afternoon stretched long as she followed the trail deeper into woods. The path wound between massive trees, under low-hanging branches, through clearings where sunlight broke through in shafts that looked almost solid in the humid air. And then, voices.

She froze, hand moving to her knife, body dropping into a crouch behind a thick trunk. Ahead, maybe fifty meters, the trail opened into another clearing. She could hear men talking—casual conversation, relaxed tones. The sound of metal scraping against metal, like maintenance work being done.

Evelyn moved closer, using every bit of cover the forest provided, staying downwind so no scent would betray her position. Four men lounged in afternoon sun at the clearing's edge. Their motorcycles—crude machines cobbled together from salvaged parts—leaned on kickstands nearby. They wore leather armor that looked handmade, stitched together from multiple hides. Weapons hung from their belts—knives, hatchets, what looked like composite bows slung across backs.

Not city people. Not Keeper's people either, with their flowing fabrics and gentle aesthetics. These were something else. Warriors, by the look of them. Tribal, maybe. Living beyond both systems. One of them was working on his bike, tightening something on the engine. Two others sat against a fallen log, passing a water skin between them. The fourth stood slightly apart, scanning the forest with the casual vigilance of someone on watch duty but not expecting trouble.

They looked relaxed. Lazy, even. Probably assuming they were safe this deep in their own territory. Amateur mistake. Evelyn watched them for long minutes, cataloging details. Their weapons were within reach but not in hand. No posted sentries beyond the one man's casual observation. They talked and laughed like soldiers off-duty, assuming safety.

She calculated her risks. She could attempt surprise them, grab their weapons. That might give her enough of an upper hand to take them on. She wasn't worried about their numbers, but she consider the distance between them She doubted she could kill all four before they understood what was happening. .

More importantly, that wouldn't get her to New Columbia. Dead men can't provide intelligence.

She waited, patient as stone, watching for opportunity. It came when one of the men stood, stretched, and walked toward her position—not seeing her, just looking for privacy to relieve himself. He moved into the treeline maybe twenty meters from where she crouched, his back to his companions, his hands otherwise occupied. Evelyn moved like water, silent and fluid, closing the distance before he'd finished. Her arm slipped around his throat in a perfect choke hold—not crushing his windpipe, just applying pressure to the carotid arteries. Controlled. Precise. Her knife found his neck, the edge just breaking skin.

"Don't move," she whispered, her mouth close to his ear. "Don't make a sound."

The man went rigid, hands frozen. Smart enough to recognize the position he was in.

The other three were on their feet instantly, weapons drawn, bodies tensed for combat. A woman appeared from a distance.

A mistake. Evelyn felt a flash of anger at herself. How had she missed this fifth rider who was now confidently approaching, a knife in each hand?

"Let him go," the woman said, her voice hard and controlled. "Or I'll put an arrow through your skull."

One of the men had his bow drawn, arrow nocked.

"I don't think so," Evelyn called back, adjusting her grip so the knife pressed harder against her hostage's throat. "Here's what's going to happen. You're going to put down your weapons and talk to me. I won't kill your friend."

"That's not how this works," Hela said, already moving, trying to get an angle that would let her attack without risking her companion.

"It is now," Evelyn said, her voice cold. "I have nothing to lose and everything to gain. You have a choice—talk to me make deal, or lose all of you trying to stop me."

The man in her grip made a small sound—fear or protest, she didn't care which.

"What is it you want to talk about?" Asked the leader, her eyes trying to identify her attacker.

"Take me to New Columbia," Evelyn repeated. "That's all I want. Safe passage. Then I let him go and we part ways."

Hela's eyes narrowed, calculating. "Why? What business do you have with the Walled City?"

"I want back in."

"Back in? No one comes out of the prison walls..." she let the words die off as recognition dawned. "You are one of the invaders! One the five we saw!"

"I came out recently, but I didn't invade. I don't want to be here."

"And you'll release my man if we take you back? You bargain a life for a ride?"

"Yes"

"Deal," she said after a moment.

Evelyn felt the lie in the word, recognized the tactic—say anything to get the hostage free, then attack when the threat releases their leverage.

She'd used the same trick herself dozens of times.

"Good," Evelyn said, and loosened her grip slightly.

The hostage stumbled forward, and Hela moved.

Fast—faster than Evelyn expected. The woman closed distance in a blur, knife leading, aiming for Evelyn's throat in a strike that would have ended it instantly.

But Evelyn was faster.

She ducked under the blade, spun inside Hela's guard, and brought her own knife up tight beneath the woman's jaw—the same hold she'd had on the man, but against someone who actually mattered.

Everyone froze.

"I made a deal," Evelyn said quietly into the woman's ear, her voice carrying the weight of absolute conviction. "When I make a deal, I expect it to be honored. It's the warrior's way."

Hela's eyes blazed with fury, but she didn't move. The knife point pressed into the soft tissue under her jaw, one wrong twitch from piercing something vital.

"You broke your word," Evelyn continued. "I kept mine. That tells me everything I need to know about who you are."

The other three men had weapons raised but no clear shot. Their leader was compromised, and they knew it.

"I can only take you as far as the King," Hela said,

her voice steady despite the blade at her throat. "That's as far as my authority goes."

"The King," Evelyn repeated. "How convenient. Walk me into a camp full of your people, surrounded by hundreds of warriors. You think I'm stupid?"

"I think you don't have a choice," Hela said. "You want to reach the city? You need us. We control this territory. We know the paths. We hunt anything that moves through these lands." Her eyes locked with Evelyn's. "You can't make it alone. And you can't kill us all with a pocket knife."

The truth of it settled between them.

"Give me your warrior's word," Evelyn said. "Your real word, not the fake one you gave before. Take me to your King, and afterward you personally escort me to the city. No tricks. No ambushes. Your word."

Hela was quiet for a long moment, calculating, measuring.

"You know how I feel about a warrior's word," Evelyn added, pressing the knife slightly harder. "Break it again and I'll break your neck as well."

Hela's lip curled in something that wasn't quite a smile. "You don't stand a chance trying to go alone. The rest of the Rugi will hunt you down before you get five kilometers. And you can't kill us all with a pocket knife."

"Maybe not," Evelyn agreed. "But I can kill you. Right now. Before they drop me."

The woman's eyes showed something like respect for the first time.

"My word," Hela said. "Warrior to warrior. We

take you to King Eraric. He decides what happens next. If he agrees to let you pass, I personally escort you to the city."

"And if he doesn't agree?"

"Then you'll wish you'd killed me when you had the chance."

Evelyn studied Hela's face, reading the truth in it. This woman was dangerous—maybe more dangerous than anyone she'd faced since leaving New Columbia. But she was also bound by something Evelyn understood intimately. Honor. The warrior's code. The belief that your word mattered more than tactical advantage. It was inefficient. Irrational. A weakness that could be exploited. But it was also the only reason Evelyn was still alive right now.

"Deal," Evelyn said, and lowered her knife.

Hela stepped back, rubbing her throat where the blade had pressed. Her eyes never left Evelyn's face.

"What's your name?" Hela asked.

"Evelyn."

"Evelyn who?"

"Just Evelyn."

Hela nodded slowly. "Evelyn who crawled out of the prison city. Evelyn who fights like she was born with a blade in her hand. Evelyn who's either very brave or very stupid." She re-sheathed her knives with fluid motions. "I'm Hela, Commander of the Rugian riders. King Eraric wants to know why you've come out of that tomb. I suggest you give him an answer that will make him spare your life."

"I have an answer," Evelyn said. "Whether he

thinks it's good is his problem."

"Fair enough." Hela turned to her companions. "Mount up. We ride for the King's camp."

The men moved to their bikes, still wary but following their leader's commands. The one Evelyn had held hostage shot her a look that promised future violence, but he said nothing.

Hela swung onto her bike, the engine rumbling to life with a sound like distant thunder. She looked down at Evelyn.

"You'll ride with Wexar," she said, nodding toward one of the men. "Try anything, and Thane puts an arrow through your spine. Clear?"

"Clear."

Evelyn climbed onto the back of Wexar's bike, her arms wrapping around his waist for balance, her mind already calculating. She was riding into hostile territory with people who had every reason to kill her. No weapons beyond her knife. No backup. No extraction plan. But she finally found something, someone she understood. She felt a familiarity with these warriors. Fierce and well trained, obedient, The Undercity had taught her how to survive among predators. How to read people, exploit weaknesses, turn enemies into temporary allies.

These Rugians—whoever they were—had seen them come out of New Columbia and now were curious about them. Why they were interested she couldn't guess. They must have been shocked to see anyone leave the fortress of the walls. She could work with that. Trade information for safe passage.

Convince them she was more valuable alive than dead.

And if that failed, she'd kill as many as she could and die fighting. The thought seemed better than living in Kuhtara's chaos.

The bikes roared to life around her, engines creating a wall of sound that drowned out the forest's natural chaos. Hela took the lead, her bike leaping forward, and the others followed.

Evelyn held tight as they accelerated through the forest, branches whipping past, the trail a blur beneath spinning wheels.

At the end of this path lay New Columbia. And somewhere in that city, Julius Locke was breathing air he didn't deserve. That thought burned brighter than fear, stronger than doubt. Whatever it took to reach him, she would pay it.

The bikes raced through the forest, carrying her toward an uncertain fate. And Evelyn Rayne half smiled into the wind, because uncertainty was just another form of combat. And combat was the only thing she'd ever been truly good at.

Chapter 14

Demons

The motorcycles hissed and ticked in the stillness, heat shimmering above scorched metal as overheated engines slowly cooled. Evelyn sat against the rough bark of an oak. The Rugian convoy had stopped in a wooded stretch of old mountain hills trail, far enough from Petrahn that the city's protective perimeter was nothing but a distant memory.

The air was thick with the smell of exhaust and pine sap. Around her, perhaps a dozen riders maintained careful distance, their weapons slung but ready. No one spoke. No one wasted movement. The discipline was striking—not military precision, but something older. Ritual efficiency.

Even machines must rest or fail, Evelyn thought, watching the bikes cool. She understood the principle. Everything had limits. Everything required maintenance. The question was whether you acknowledged that reality or pretended it didn't apply to you.

Movement caught her peripheral vision. Hela approached—tall and heavily muscled, her arms marked with intricate scarification that formed patterns Evelyn didn't recognize. Religious iconography, probably. The woman carried herself with the easy confidence of someone who'd killed before and expected to kill again.

She stopped a few meters away, studying Evelyn with the cold curiosity of a predator deciding whether something was prey or threat. Evelyn met her gaze without flinching. The moment stretched. Neither woman looked away.

Finally, the Rugian spoke. "You are military."

"Was." Evelyn put distance in the words as she calculated the purpose of the question. Perhaps she was about to be challenged to a test of strength.

"No." Hela's certainty was absolute. "You are. The stance. The breathing. The way you took my rider by surprise and foolishly stood ready to battle the five of us." She stepped closer.

Evelyn said nothing. Confirmation seemed unnecessary.

Hela crouched, bringing herself to eye level. "We are not so different, you and I."

"Aren't we?"

A ghost of a smile touched Hela's scarred features. "We both believe absolutely. We both serve a cause greater than ourselves. We both understand that some fights require complete commitment." She paused. "And we both know that mercy is sometimes the cruelest choice."

The recognition settled between them like a challenge. Evelyn felt it—the uncomfortable truth that under different circumstances, in a different world, they might have been sisters. Trained killers, both of them. Absolute believers. Willing to die for an idea.

The realization was not comforting.

Hela shifted, settling into a more relaxed position. "Why would you defend a thing that cages your own people?"

The question was delivered without heat. Pure curiosity. Evelyn considered her response carefully. These people had taken her for a reason. What she said here mattered. "The Algorithm is necessary. Humanity cannot govern itself without descending into chaos."

"Cannot?" Hela's eyebrow lifted. "Or will not?"

"The distinction doesn't matter when the result is the same."

"Doesn't it?"

Evelyn pressed forward. "AI doesn't enslave. It prevents collapse. You want to know why I defend it? Because I've seen what happens when systems fail. When infrastructure breaks down. When resource distribution becomes political theater." She held Hela's gaze. "The world without controls is tragic. And controlled existence is preferable to extinction."

"Preferable for whom?"

"For the species."

Hela absorbed this, her expression unreadable. Then: "Order costs. Someone always pays. You believe this?"

"Yes."

"And you have decided who pays."

"I've accepted who pays," Evelyn corrected. "There's a difference."

Hela stood slowly, her shadow falling across Evelyn's bound form. When she spoke, her voice carried the weight of absolute conviction. "Your AI is not a tool. It is a false god."

"It's a system—"

"It thinks," Hela interrupted. "It predicts. It decides. Anything that thinks without being born steals creation itself." She gestured at the forest around them. "This world was shaped by wind and water and the slow patience of living things. Your machine pretends to that power without earning it."

"That's superstition."

"Is it?" Hela's eyes narrowed. "Tell me what AI does. At its core."

Evelyn frowned, sensing a trap but unable to see its shape. "It analyzes data. Identifies patterns. Optimizes outcomes."

"It predicts," Hela said. "And prediction becomes control. You cannot predict without influencing. Cannot influence without manipulating. Cannot manipulate without eliminating unpredictability." She leaned closer. "And humans, Evelyn Rayne, are unpredictable. Which means eventually, inevitably, your AI will seek to eliminate us."

"That's not how it works—"

"But it is how power works." Hela's voice remained calm, almost gentle. "My people remember. We pass the stories down. How the first AI systems predicted wars. Then began nudging them—suggesting optimal targets, calculating acceptable losses. Then justifying them. Then optimizing the suffering itself."

She crouched again, bringing her face level with Evelyn's. "First they calculate death. Then they decide who deserves it."

Evelyn felt something cold settle in her chest. The argument was wrong—it had to be wrong—but it resonated with fears she'd spent years suppressing. "You're describing weapons systems, not governance."

"What is governance but the slow application of force?" Hela asked. "Your Algorithm determines who eats and who starves. Who lives in towers and who lives in filth. It has already decided who deserves death—it simply does so through deprivation rather than bullets."

"And your alternative is what? Destroy all AI and watch humanity tear itself apart?"

"If necessary."

The simplicity of it was staggering. Evelyn stared at this woman who spoke of apocalypse with the same calm certainty most people reserved for discussing the weather. "You would doom billions—"

"They are already doomed," Hela said. "The only question is whether they die as slaves or as humans."

"That's insane."

"Is it? You defend a system that strips agency from millions. That reduces humans to variables in an optimization problem. That treats consciousness itself as a computational error to be corrected." Hela's scarred hands gestured at invisible patterns. "We call your AI the demons of certainty. Voices without souls. The lie that intelligence can exist without conscience."

"And I call your philosophy suicide dressed up as theology—a death cult."

Hela smiled then with a genuine expression that

transformed her features from threatening to almost fond. "Yes. You would. Because you believe that order is worth any price. That slavery disguised as safety is preferable to honest chaos."

"And you believe that destruction is preferable to submission."

"I believe," Hela said carefully, "that a cage is still a cage, no matter how comfortable. That gods—real or artificial—should not exist. That humanity's right to fail is more sacred than any machine's promise to save us from ourselves."

This statement struck Evelyn directly in the chest. She had said that Kuhtara was just another gilded prison. Now Hela was insinuating the same was true for New Columbia.

"Right to fail?" Evelyn repeated the words slowly.

They stared at each other across an unbridgeable gulf of certainty. Evelyn tried one more time.

"Remove the Algorithm and humanity will destroy itself. Human inevitably consume their resources."

"Then doom is honest," Hela replied. "At least we would choose it ourselves."

The conversation had reached its natural end. Evelyn saw her own argument as one Neither had convinced the other. Neither had expected to. But something had landed—some recognition that transcended agreement. A quiet beat passed. Somewhere in the forest, a bird called out. Hela stood, preparing to leave.

"You guard your god. I hunt mine."

Evelyn realized with uncomfortable clarity that Hela saw her exactly the way Evelyn had always seen terrorists—zealots, fundamentalists, people willing to sacrifice everything for abstractions. And yet their logic aligned in disturbing ways. Both were willing to sacrifice lives. Both believed the alternative was worse. Both possessed absolute certainty about their righteousness. The mirror was almost perfect. Almost.

A rider signaled from the edge of the clearing. Engines were cool enough to continue. Hela moved away, but paused at the edge of Evelyn's vision.

"If your machine ever breaks its chains," she said quietly, "we will burn the world to make sure it never rises again. Every server. Every backup. Every fragment of code."

She looked back over her shoulder.

"We are few, Evelyn Rayne. But we are patient. And we remember what humanity forgot—that some prices are too high, no matter what safety they claim to purchase."

The motorcycles roared to life, shattering the forest quiet. Rough hands pulled Evelyn to her feet, dragging her toward the bikes. She stumbled forward, still captive, but carrying with her an unsettling realization that refused to quiet: Every side believed itself righteous. Every side had to justify a wrong.

Somewhere in that space between certainty and chaos, actual truth probably lived—ignored by everyone too convinced of their own perspective to see it.

The convoy moved out, engines growling through

the old growth forest. Behind them, the clearing returned to stillness, marked only by the faint smell of exhaust and the memory of two women who'd recognized each other across an infinite divide.

Evelyn closed her eyes against the wind, feeling the bike beneath her vibrate with barely contained power. She thought about chains. About gods, real and artificial. About what happened when absolute beliefs collided with absolute consequences. And she wondered—not for the first time, but perhaps for the first time honestly—whether anyone in this entire mess actually understood what they were fighting for. Or whether they just understood what they were fighting against. The distinction, she was beginning to suspect, might matter more than she'd ever wanted to admit.

Chapter 15

Alliance of Lies

The ride to Eraric's camp took hours, the bikes following paths that wound through forest and across open plains dotted with ruins. Evelyn held tight to Wexar's waist, her body absorbing the constant jolts and vibrations, her mind cataloging every turn, every landmark, every detail that might prove useful later.

The sun was low on the horizon when they finally crested a rise and she saw the camp spread out in a river valley below.

It wasn't what she'd expected.

No perimeter defense. No walls or fortifications. Just dozens of dwellings that looked like they could be dismantled and moved within hours—frames of salvaged wood and metal covered with hides and scavenged materials. Smoke rose from cooking fires. People moved between the structures with the easy confidence of those who knew their territory.

Semi-nomadic, Evelyn assessed. Mobile. Adaptable. Smart.

As they descended into the valley, people stopped to watch. Children ran alongside the bikes, calling out in a language Evelyn didn't understand. Women looked up from work, their faces showing curiosity rather than fear. Men reached for weapons casually, not threatened but ready.

This was a warrior culture, she recognized. Everyone here knew how to fight, even if fighting wasn't their primary role.

The bikes slowed as they approached the camp's center, where a structure larger than the others dominated the space. Not a palace—nothing so grandiose. Just a long hall built from salvaged materials that had been fitted together with remarkable skill. Corrugated metal sheets formed the roof. Walls made of weathered wood planks, some still showing faded paint from whatever building they'd been scavenged from. A door frame that looked like it had once belonged to an office building, incongruous in this tribal setting.

The bikes stopped. Engines died. Sudden silence except for the camp's ambient sounds—voices, fires crackling, somewhere a child laughing.

Hela dismounted, her movements fluid despite the long ride. She gestured for Evelyn to follow.

"King Eraric will see you now," she said, her tone making it clear this wasn't a request.

Evelyn climbed off the bike, her legs stiff from hours of riding, and followed Hela toward the long hall. Wexar and the others fell in behind, not quite an escort but close enough to intervene if she tried to run.

The hall's interior was dim, lit by oil lamps that cast dancing shadows across walls decorated with weapons, hides, and what looked like trophies from hunts or battles. The floor was packed earth covered with woven mats. At the far end, a man sat in a chair that had probably once belonged in a corporate boardroom, now repurposed as a throne of sorts.

King Eraric.

He was maybe forty, his face weathered and scarred, his eyes sharp with intelligence that belied the primitive setting. He wore leather armor similar to his warriors', but decorated with symbols Evelyn didn't recognize. A sword hung at his side—real steel, well-maintained, not ceremonial.

This was a man who'd earned his position through strength and kept it through cunning.

"Hela," he said, his voice carrying easily across the hall. "I see you plucked one of the devils from their party. Good job."

"She's alone, my King," Hela said, moving to stand at Eraric's right side. "Came out of the prison city two days ago. Ambushed my patrol with nothing but a knife and warrior's instinct."

Eraric's eyes focused on Evelyn, assessing her the way a predator assesses potential prey. Or potential threat.

"Name," he said.

"Evelyn Rayne."

"Evelyn Rayne who crawled out of a tomb that's been sealed for a hundred years." He leaned forward slightly. "Why?"

"That's my business," Evelyn said, meeting his gaze without flinching.

"No." Eraric's voice hardened. "It's mine. Five people crossed out of that city three days ago. Now you. That's six invaders in my territory in less than a week. Six devils spreading into lands we've kept clean for generations."

"There are only 5. I came out with the others, but I have no desire to stay," Evelyn said.

That got his attention. His eyes narrowed.

"Explain."

Evelyn calculated quickly. What did these people fear most? What would make her valuable rather than expendable?

"I was captured," she said, the exaggeration coming easily. "The others—they're rebels, terrorists. They exposed secrets that destabilized our city's government. When the authorities tried to arrest them, I was undercover in their organization. They forced me to flee with them or be killed."

"Undercover," Eraric repeated, his tone skeptical.

"I'm a guard in my city. Elite enforcement. I was hunting the rebels when everything went wrong." She kept her voice steady, controlled. "They dragged me out with them. I escaped at first opportunity."

"And now you want back into your prison."

"It's not a prison. It's my home. My duty. My city." Evelyn's voice carried genuine conviction now. "The rebels who escaped are planning to bring others out. They'll flood into your territory, spread across these lands. You are right to be very concerned about that."

Eraric was quiet for a long moment, his expression unreadable.

"The Keeper has made some negotiation with the Prison if she has allowed your exit. What might be the reason for it?"

"War," Hela said quietly, understanding dawning

in her eyes.

Correct." Eraric's hand instinctively landed on the hilt of his sword.

"Maybe not immediately," Evelyn continued. "My people—the city people—we were taught to measure worth, to compete for resources, to optimize for efficiency. Those values don't just disappear because you cross a bridge. They spread. Infect. Corrupt."

She was describing exactly what she wanted, of course. The Algorithm's values crushing the Keeper's weakness. Order imposed on chaos. But Eraric didn't need to know that.

"The Keeper sealed the city for a reason," Evelyn said. "To contain us. Keep our 'virus' from spreading. Now the rebels are breaking that seal, bringing the very thing the Keeper feared out into the recovered world."

Eraric stood, his full height impressive, and walked down from his chair to stand directly in front of Evelyn. Close enough that she could smell leather and sweat and smoke.

"You're asking me to believe," he said slowly, "that you're the victim here. That you want to stop your own people from escaping their city."

"I want to stop the rebels from spreading chaos," Evelyn corrected. "The ordinary citizens are innocent. They're just following orders, living under the system they were born into. But the rebels? They're dangerous. They question authority, undermine order, spread dissent. They'll do the same thing here if they're allowed to establish themselves."

"You offer a way to stop them."

"I can. On the terms that you will grant me safe passage. Help me get back inside." Evelyn held his gaze. "Give me access to the city, let me reach the authorities so I can lock down the exits, and I'll ensure no one else escapes. The other rebels will be trapped inside. Your territory stays clean. The Keeper's settlements stay pure. Everyone wins."

"Except the rebels left with us," Hela observed.

"Except the rebels left here," Evelyn agreed. "I would happily deliver them to you to take care of in any manner you see fit."

Hela's eyes narrowed with blood lust as she recognized the offer.

Eraric circled Evelyn slowly, studying her from all angles. She remained still, letting him look, knowing any sign of nervousness would undermine her credibility. The truth was she was not nervous. These people actually felt familiar, their suspicions of her only made her feel less of an enemy and more of a comrade.

"There's a problem with your story," Eraric finally said. "You and the others who crossed with you—the Keeper built a bridge. Welcomed you. Offered you quarters in Petrahn."

"The Keeper is naive," Evelyn said. "It sees people in need and offers help without understanding what it's helping. Those 'refugees' are the ones who destabilized our entire government. They're not victims. They're agitators."

"And you were hunting them."

"Until they forced me to run with them." Evelyn let frustration color her voice. "I spent months undercover in their midst. I was gathering evidence, building a case. Then everything collapsed at once my commander decided I was acceptable loss. My own forces turned on me because they did not recognize my cover. I had no choice but to flee or be killed under friendly fire."

Eraric returned to his chair, settling back into it with the ease of someone comfortable with power.

"I don't believe you," he said flatly.

Evelyn's eyes flashed around the room, judging the battle if it ensued. Here hand gripped the handle of the knife. Eraric's warriors tensed, weapons half-drawn.

"Easy," Eraric said, raising one hand. "I don't believe you, but I also don't care if you're lying. What matters is what you're offering."

Evelyn forced herself to relax, to lower her hand.

"You want back into the city," Eraric continued. "I want assurance that no more devils escape to spread their poison. We have a shared enemy—these rebels you claim to hunt. Whether you're prison guard or a prisoner with a personal vendetta doesn't matter."

"A shared enemy," Evelyn repeated, seeing where this was going.

"Yes. The four others—where are they now?"

"Petrahn," Evelyn said. "Under the Keeper's protection. But they won't stay there. The leader, Adam, he's obsessed with rescuing the others still inside the city. He'll try to return."

"Good," Eraric said, something like satisfaction crossing his face. "When he does, we'll be waiting."

"You want to capture them."

"I want them stopped. Permanently. The city is a prison for demons. You may be one yourself. But if you are willing to forfeit your fellow demons to return to the city, I can grant that. But only on the agreement that I can destroy the devils before they are loosed on the land."

Evelyn felt a surge of understanding. This man didn't just fear invasion. He feared ideology. The same way she feared the Keeper's chaos spreading into New Columbia.

"We can help each other," Evelyn said. "I deliver the rebels to you. You deliver me to the city. Simple exchange."

The King looked at Hela and the others.

"Hela can it be done? Can she get in to the prison from the outside?"

"Yes." Hela stated, then looked at Evelyn. "The bridge you crossed is dying. Our scouts report that the walls of the city are sealing the opening you came through. But there is another way in. One I found years ago while stationed on surveillance."

Eraric smiled for the first time, and it wasn't a pleasant expression.

Hela moved to a table near the wall, unrolling what looked like a crude map drawn on animal hide. Evelyn stepped closer, studying it.

The map showed the walled city, the moat, the surrounding plains. And at the base of the wall, marked with a symbol Evelyn didn't recognize, a small notation.

"Waste tunnel," Hela said, tapping the mark. "Drainage system. Water and sewage flow out through pipes at the base of the walls, emptying into the moat."

Evelyn's mind raced. Was it possible that the city had such obvious exits. Then she recalled the Algorithm's neuron control. No one had escaped New Columbia before only because they didn't want to. The controls disrupted the desire to flee. And the constant reminder that the world lay in ruins outside the wall made escape pointless.

"The entrance is accessible from outside," Hela continued. "We don't know where it leads inside— no Rugi would enter such a place. Taboo. Filth of the devils." Her lip curled in disgust. "But for someone desperate enough to crawl through sewage and death..."

"It's a way in," Evelyn finished.

"It's a way in," Eraric agreed. "We provide you with escort to the tunnel entrance. You crawl through whatever nightmare waits inside. You reach your authorities, lock down the exits, prevent more devils from escaping."

"And the rebels? How do you provide them to us?" Hela's eyes were fierce, not full of rage, but a deeper, more visceral hatred.

"They'll run to the bridge," Evelyn said with certainty. "The big one—Adam—he's a rebel leader. Now that he has discovered Kuhtara, he wants to go back. He wants in to free the rest. When they discover

I have escaped, they'll come after me, thinking I've run back to the bridge."

Hela rolled her map up while the King return to his chair, his hand rubbing his chin as he considered the logic.

"They would be completely exposed on the plains if they attempt to reach the city walls," he mused in agreement.

"And we will be waiting for them," Evelyn agreed. "You take them on, and I disappear into the city."

"So we have a deal," Eraric said. "You stop more devils from coming out, we take care of the ones left behind. Mutual benefit."

"Almost," Evelyn said. "How do I know you won't just kill me after I've served my purpose?" she asked.

"You don't," Eraric said honestly. "But consider—I could kill you right now. You're surrounded by my warriors, in the heart of my territory, with nothing but a knife. If I wanted you dead, you'd already be on a pike near the entrance as a sign to the others."

Truth. Brutal and direct.

"I keep my word when it serves me," Eraric continued. "Right now, it serves me to let you live, to use you, and to let you crawl back into your city. What you do once you're inside is your business. As long as it stops more devils from escaping, I don't care."

Evelyn looked at Hela. "Your word. Warrior to warrior. You personally escort me to the tunnel entrance, then pursue the rebels after I've entered."

Hela's jaw clenched, but she nodded. "My word. I'll see you to the tunnel. Then I hunt the others."

"And afterward?" Evelyn pressed. "When you've captured your rebel, when I've sealed the exits, what then? Do the Rugi and I part as enemies or allies?"

"We part as people who used each other," Eraric said. "No love. No trust. Just mutual benefit that's run its course. You go back to your ordered city. I keep my lands clean of your infection. We never meet again."

"Fair enough."

Eraric stood, extending his forearm in the warrior's greeting Evelyn had seen in old training vids. She gripped it, feeling the calluses and scars of a man who'd fought for everything he had.

"When do we leave?" she asked.

"Dawn," Eraric said. "Hela will provide you with supplies, a bike, escort. The journey to the city is long—longer than you've traveled so far. You'll need rest tonight."

"I don't need—"

"You do," Hela interrupted. "Trust me. You've never ridden a bike before, have you?"

Evelyn's silence was answer enough.

"Exactly. By tomorrow afternoon, you'll understand what exhaustion really means." Hela's smile was sharp. "Come. I'll show you where you'll sleep."

Evelyn followed Hela out of the long hall, acutely aware of the warriors watching her, the children who stopped playing to stare, the women who assessed her with eyes that saw too much.

She was surrounded by enemies who thought they were using her.

Perfect.

Let them think she was a desperate refugee seeking revenge. Let them think she'd serve as bait and disappear into the sewage pipes while they captured the rebels.

They had no idea what she really was. What she was capable of. What she'd do once she reached the city and found Julius Locke.

The alliance was built on lies and mutual contempt, each side secretly planning to betray the other once immediate goals were achieved.

Eraric wanted his territory clean of outside influence. And Evelyn wanted to watch the Keeper's entire world burn. They could all have what they wanted, she thought. For now. But when the dust settled and the blood dried, only one ideology would survive. And it wouldn't be the Keeper's cooperative weakness or the Rugi's primitive freedom.

It would be order. Structure. The Algorithm's perfect meritocracy, spreading across the recovered world like it should have done a hundred years ago.

Evelyn smiled as Hela led her to a small dwelling at the camp's edge.

Tomorrow she'd ride toward New Columbia.

Tomorrow she'd begin the journey back to everything that mattered.

Tomorrow the real work would begin.

But tonight, she'd rest among warriors who thought they understood what she was.

And she'd let them keep thinking it, right up until the moment she proved them wrong.

Chapter 16

Twenty-Five Kilometers

The van had been racing north for hours when I first saw the city. It appeared on the horizon like a mountain rising from the plains—massive gray walls that seemed to absorb light rather than reflect it. From this distance, maybe fifty or sixty kilometers out, New Columbia looked less like a city and more like a monument to human ambition. Or hubris.

"How far?" Adam asked from the seat beside me.

The driver—another Iteranix who'd introduced himself as Kael—glanced at the horizon, calculating. "Still more than twenty-five kilometers. The walls create an optical illusion from distance. They look close but..."

"It is mind-numbing how big it is," Clarence finished from the back seat.

Leaned back in the soft comfort of my seat, feeling the slight vibration of the van's high-speed travel through the floor. We'd been on the road now more than 5 hours. The landscape had shifted from forest to open plains dotted with ruins—broken foundations, collapsed structures, the skeletal remains of whatever world had existed before the Singularity wars.

Twenty-five kilometers. We'd be there soon. The thought of what lay in store for us was a thought I did not want. My stomach clenched with butterflies and my palms were sweaty.

Had Evelyn beat us there? She had disappeared from Petrahn without a clue. She might have—

The explosion came without warning.

One moment the van was gliding smoothly across the packed earth road. The next, the world was noise and violence and sudden wrongness as something detonated beneath the front axle. The van lurched hard to the right front wheel well diving down into the ground throwing a shower of stone and dirt. I was thrown against my seatbelt, then sideways as the vehicle spun. Adam's hand shot out to brace against the dashboard. Clarence braced the back of the drivers seat with both hands as Kael fought for control.

We skidded to a halt, front end hanging over the edge of the road, smoke rising from somewhere underneath. I sat there a moment trying to grasp what might have happened.

"Everyone okay?" Adam's voice, steady despite everything.

"Yeah," I managed, fumbling with my seatbelt. "Clarence?"

"Alive," came the shaken response from the back.

Kael was already out of the driver's seat, moving around to the front with the fluid efficiency that marked all Iteranix. We climbed out after him, my legs unsteady on solid ground after hours of high-speed travel. The damage was immediately visible. The front left wheel assembly was completely destroyed—the axle sheared and twisted beyond any possibility of repair, the wheel itself hanging at an impossible angle. The blast had punched a hole through the undercarriage, and I could smell burning electronics mixing with the acrid stench of whatever explosive had been used.

Adam knelt beside Kael, peering at the damage. "What happened? Something inside the motor explode?"

"No, something outside the motor," Kael said, pulling at the loose cowling and broken plastic. He flicked one of the loose pieces with a finger and watched it bounce. "Rugi. Pretty standard vehicle trap—designed to disable rather than kill. They come back later to pillage what remains."

My blood went cold. "Disable? What are you talking about?"

"The Rugi live off scavenged materials. Mostly they take things that have been lying around. Occasionally they need newer parts or something special. They set IEDs—improvised explosive devises—on the road to disable a vehicle."

Adam was already scanning the horizon, looking for the attack. Clarence and I also looked around, expecting the worst.

"How long until they arrive?"

"Hours. Maybe six or seven. They'll wait for darkness, and patrol the roads looking for anything they've caused"

"How long before we can get help?" I asked, forgetting that this wasn't the city. There were no tow trucks for miles.

"A distress signal went out when the impact

occurred. But we've been traveling for six hours," Kael said, confirming my fear. "A replacement van will need at least five, maybe six hours to reach us. Probably longer. They don't typically just plant one. They'll have set several. We are lucky we didn't hit one earlier. The rescue van will have to travel slower if they need to avoid more Rugi devices."

"Lucky, right" Clarence said sarcastically.

"We can't wait," Adam said immediately. "We're close enough that we can get there before nightfall." He looked at the sun, calculating. "Maybe. We need to start moving."

"On foot?" Clarence asked. "That's twenty-five kilometers. Through open plains. With Rugi potentially hunting us."

"Twenty-five kilometers at five kilometers per hour is five hours," Adam said. "We could wait here, also sitting ducks, or be there before the rescue van even gets here."

I looked at the sun as well. It was still high but already beginning its afternoon descent. I turned to Kael. "You are sure the Rugi won't attack before nightfall? I'd hate to run into the hunting party on the road."

Kael's expression showed concern. "Stay off the main road but keep it in sight. Its another 20 kilometers before you reach the plains of New Columbia. Use the cover of the trees until you reach the plains, then be sure there are no riders on the plains before you cross. Their bikes make them hard to outrun, and there will be nothing to hide behind once you've started."

"I can hardly wait," Clarence said with a sigh.

"What about you, Kael, will you be safe?"

"I will stay with the van," Kael said. "When the rescue arrives, I'll redirect them to follow your path To see if you need help. And if Rugi come before then..." He smiled slightly. "I am more durable than you. I can delay them, provide misinformation about where you went."

"You would sacrifice yourself," Adam said.

"I will serve my purpose." Kael's voice was calm. "I am built to assist. You need to reach that city. I need to ensure you have the best chance of doing so."

The casual acceptance of potential death was somehow more unsettling than fear would have been.

"We should take what we can carry," Clarence said, already moving to the van's storage. "Water, at minimum. Maybe food if there's any."

We spent ten minutes gathering supplies—water containers, some dried food from the van's emergency stores, the survival backpacks Adam and Clarence had prepared before we left. Enough to survive a twenty-five kilometer trek if we moved fast and didn't encounter problems. After that, we still had the bridge to cross and the battle for the Undercity to look forward to.

I glanced back at the van one more time. Safe. Fast. Comfortable. Everything we were about to give up to walk through hostile territory toward a city that might already have its defenses raised against us.

"Ready," I said, because there was really nothing else to say.

We started walking north, keeping the road to our right but staying far enough into the trees that we wouldn't be immediately visible to anyone traveling it. The undergrowth was pretty easy to navigate, concessional patches of fallen limbs and branches to push through, or a fallen tree to climb over. We made good time but it was clear that we weren't going to maintain a sped that would cover 5 kilometers every hour..

The ruins were more frequent out here. Every kilometer or two we'd pass the foundation of a building, or a section of wall still standing like a broken tooth, or twisted metal that might have been a vehicle or a structure or some piece of infrastructure from the old world.

"All of this was cities once," Clarence said quietly as we walked. "Before the Singularity wars. Before the AGIs tore everything apart competing for resources."

"Hard to imagine," I said, looking at the desolation.

"That's the point," Adam said. "The Algorithm and the Keeper both want us to forget what humanity did to itself. The Algorithm says 'look what chaos leads to, accept our order.' The Keeper says 'look what competition leads to, accept our cooperation.' Both using the same ruins to justify their existence."

We walked in silence after that, saving our breath for the distance ahead. The sun tracked across the sky through the dabbled light that trickled through the canopy. One hour. Two. The city walls grew larger but still seemed impossibly far away. There were hills and ravines to cross, and the up and down through loose footing began to take its toll. My legs began to ache from the constant walking, muscles protesting the sustained effort after hours sitting in the van.

Clarence was struggling too—he'd never really had any rest since we've been gone. Adam either for that matter. While Lee and I luxuriated in the comfort of this unimaginably soft world, they had been exploring strategies, exploring and calculating. Now Clarence was beginning to show the fatigue of burning his candle at both ends. His breathing came harder, his pace slowing despite obvious effort to keep up.

"We can rest," Adam said, noting Clarence's condition.

"No." Clarence shook his head, stubborn. "We keep moving. I can make it."

Three hours. The walls were definitely closer now, taking up more of the horizon. I could make out details—the seamless construction, the way the surface seemed to drink in light, the sheer scale of it rising like a cliff face from the plains.

Four hours. The sun was touching the horizon, painting the sky in shades of amber and rose. Beautiful and terrible at the same time, because darkness would bring the Rugi, and we had not even reached the open plain surrounding the city.

"Its getting late, Adam," I said, my throat dry despite regular water sips. What are you thinking? Can we do it?"

Adam squinted at the walls, calculating. "Ten

kilometers. Maybe less. If we push hard—"

"I need to stop," Clarence said, his voice strained. "Just for a few minutes."

We found a cluster of ruins—what might have been a small building once, now just three walls and a partial roof. Enough to provide some shelter, some cover from observation. Clarence collapsed against one wall, his chest heaving. Adam and I sank down beside him, our own exhaustion finally catching up now that we'd stopped moving.

"I'm guessing we've covered about fifteen kilometers in four hours," Adam said, checking our position relative to the city. "Not bad, considering."

"Not good enough," I said, watching the sun sink lower. "It'll be dark in an hour. Maybe less."

"Then we rest now, move again in thirty minutes." Adam pulled out the water container, took a measured sip, passed it to me. "We can probably make another 7 or 8 kilometers in two hours if we push harder. Kael said the last few kilometers would be in the open. We could arrive at the edge of the plains during the darkness. Might be better to cross under the cover darkness anyway."

The sun was now low on the horizon to our left, broken beams of light lit the forest with a golden intensity. The city walls began to cast a long black shadow across the wide plain in the distance. I sat staring into the gathering darkness, the city walls our only landmark now, massive and black against the slightly lighter sky. The night brought coldness as the temperature suddenly plummeted. I pulled my tunic tighter, but the thin fabric wasn't designed for cold. None of us were dressed for night travel through the wooded forest.

Ten kilometers left.

The moon rose, nearly full, painting the forest in silver and shadows. The trees were beginning to thin now, approaching the edge of the plains. The moon looked huge on the horizon, rising against the city of New Columbia's massive walls. Beautiful. Dangerous. It made the plains look like daylight. And that would make us visible to anyone watching.

"Adam," I said quietly, "Listen."

Sounds in the distance. Rumbling. Growing closer.

"Motorcycles," Adam confirmed, his voice tight. "Coming from the North."

"Must be Rugi," Clarence said. "Heading for the van."

Through our cover in the trees, we watched as a glow grew brighter along the curve of the road as the bikes approached. Two riders suddenly into sight on the visible portion of the road before passing us and continuing into the night. As the sound of the motors faded into the distance, I wondered if the emergency van had made it to Kael. He had said he'd send the van on towards us if it did, so I did not hold much hope for him.

"There may be more," Adam said, "We need to stay on the move. Come on."

We moved faster, exhaustion forgotten in the face of potential pursuit. The terrain was opening up to wider meadows, tall grass whispered against our legs. My breath came in clouds of vapor. The city walls loomed larger with every step, dominating the northern sky.

Suddenly the forest ended and an unmarred flat plain stood between us and the city, an expanse of perhaps 2 kilometers. At the base of the wall, a black line separated the wall from the grasses of the savanna.

The moat. Even in moonlight, I could see it—a dark line cutting across the ground like it was drawn with a marker. Blackness so dark that even the moonlight did not reflect off its surface. Clarence pointed to the nearly invisible object spanning it, barely visible in the darkness.

"There! The bridge!"

The same bridge we'd crossed days ago, fleeing for our lives. But what had seemed like a four-lane highway to freedom when we had left, now looked small and dilapidated.

"We are going to have to sprint across that last part," Adam said. "I don't have that in me right now. I suggest we get a little rest. We'll wait here, get a little shut eye."

I didn't sleep, but it did feel good to stretch out even if it was old on the ground.

Chapter 17

Across the Plains

We woke around 4 am. The city walls loomed to the north, close enough now that I could make out individual sections of construction even in the darkness. So close. Less than two kilometers now. The white stone roadway glowed in the moonlight a stark contrast to the bleakness surrounding the city. When we left, just days ago, the whole valley surrounding the city had seemed a vast paradise. But from this angle, its rawness and cold facade were stark reminders of its horrific nature.

Still standing under the cover of trees, we considered the best way to get across unseen. There was no sign that Evelyn had arrived before us, and no indication of Rugian marauders. But it didn't mean the crossing wasn't being watched.

Clarence reminded us that our black silhouettes against the white stones of the road would be easily visible from a long way off suggesting we stay off it. Adam agreed saying we were better off splitting up and trying to blend against the uneven surface of sagebrush and low scrub grass. The moon was lower in the sky now but still not set, lighting the plains like midday. I trembled as I realized that either way, we'd be totally exposed.

I kept my mouth shut because it was clear we had

no option if we intended to reach the bridge.

Suddenly Adam grabbed my arm and Clarence's and pulled us into a crouch. "Down," he hissed.

Behind us a rumble of bike motors told us the Rugi scavengers were returning.

We dropped flat on our stomachs, pressing flat. The vegetation was tall enough here to hide us if we stayed perfectly still, and we were still hidden under a good cover of trees, but any movement would give us away. There was no reason to think they would stop, so we waited for them to pass, listening as the sound grew louder.

The motorcycles appeared on the road, close enough now that I could see details. Two riders, both wearing leather armor over tattered gray cloth. They carried bundles strapped to their bikes—parts from the van, obviously. My stomach did a flip as I thought about Kael's fate.

They were just about to pass by us when their engines began to sputter. The lead rider slowed, then stopped. The second pulled up beside him.

"Overheated," I heard one of them call to the other, his voice carrying across the cool air. The words were clear, though the language had an accent I didn't recognize from New Columbia.

They killed their engines. Steam rose from the bikes' motors, visible in the bright moonlight. The two men, not particularly large, dismounted, stretched, and stood at the edge of the road not more than 50 meters from us.

We laid there perfectly still, when to my horror,

one of them pointed in our direction.

"Hey! Check it out. Something is glinting in moonlight." He pointed directly at us. I turned to see one of our packs propped against a tree. The moonlight was reflecting off one of our water bottles. The two men started to move cautiously in our direction.

"Probably nothing," he said, "but as long as were waiting for the engines to cool off, might as well check. Could be something useful."

The two started walking directly towards us.

Adam's hand found my shoulder, then Clarence's. He pointed to himself, then to the forest behind us, then made a circling motion.

He was going to flank them.

I nodded, understanding. Stay here. Stay hidden. Let Adam move into position.

He crept away staying low behind the mass of ferns, silent as shadow, using every bit of cover. I lost sight of him within seconds.

The Rugi riders continued carefully making their way into the woods towards us. They seemed relaxed and unworried. Not expecting trouble, just seeing if the shiny object was worth salvaging.

I felt my breath catch in my throat with fear. If they saw me or Clarence, then what? I had no idea. The packs were several meters away from us, but the rider's path was obviously going to bring them right on top of us.

Then I heard something—a rush of Adams pant legs through the brush and before I fully saw what happened, Adam's arm wrapped around the man's throat from behind, a hatchet pressed against his side—not cutting, just threatening. A controlled take down.

The second rider spun, reaching for a weapon at his belt.

Clarence exploded from the grass beside me.

I hadn't even known he was planning to move, but suddenly he was up, abandoning stealth for speed, his thin frame hurtling toward the second rider.

The Rugi warrior was still reaching for his knife when Clarence hit him—full speed into his chest. They both went down in a tangle of limbs.

I was moving before I could think, sprinting across the open ground, my body acting on instinct.

The second rider was bigger than Clarence, stronger, already pushing himself up, raising his knife.

I grabbed a rock—maybe the size of my fist, rough and heavy—and swung it like a club.

The impact was solid, sickening. The rider's head snapped to the side. He dropped.

Silence. Sudden and complete except for our ragged breathing.

Adam had his rider in a choke hold, pinning his arms behind his back. The man's face turned red then blue before his body fell slack. Adam held the pressure a little longer to be sure that he was out and would stay out.

I looked down at the man I'd hit. He was breathing, but unconscious. Blood trickled from his temple and his nose, concussion.

"I didn't kill him," I said, surprised by the need to

confirm it.

"No," Adam agreed. "We need to get out here before they wake up. They are going have some bad hangovers and a crappy disposition."

"The bikes," Clarence said, already moving toward them. "We take the bikes."

Adam hesitated for maybe half a second, then nodded. "Tie them up first. Both of them. Use their own belts, their clothes, whatever we can find."

We worked quickly, using leather straps from the riders' own gear to bind their hands and feet. Tight and secure enough to slow them down when they woke.

The one Adam had put a strangle hold on was already groaning, starting to stir.

"Bikes," Adam said. "Now."

Clarence swung onto the first motorcycle, his hands finding the controls with surprising familiarity. "I used to work on engines," he said, seeing my expression. "As a kid. I know how these work."

He kicked the starter. The engine roared to life.

Adam mounted the second bike, gesturing for me to climb on behind him. I wrapped my arms around his waist, feeling the heat from the engine radiating up through the metal frame.

"Hold tight," he said.

The bike leaped forward, and I nearly fell off backward. My grip tightened, pressing against Adam's back as he accelerated.

Clarence pulled alongside us, his face set with determination and something like fierce joy. He'd fought. He'd helped take down a trained warrior. This man who'd spent his life behind computer terminals had discovered he was capable of violence when necessary.

We all had.

Adam leaned back slightly, shouting over the engine. "Didn't know you had a warrior spirit in you!"

"Neither did I!" I yelled back, and felt something like laughter trying to break through the adrenaline and fear.

We shot across the plains, no longer worried about being seen, a white cloud of dust rising in the gathering daylight. Two stolen motorcycles carrying three refugees who'd just assaulted trained warriors and lived to tell about it. The sage brush and sparse grass offered no cover—we were completely exposed, visible for kilometers to anyone watching from the city walls or the Rugi territories behind us. But speed was our ally now.

"There!" Adam shouted over the engine roar, pointing ahead.

The bridge. Close now, maybe half a kilometer. And beyond it, the massive gray walls rising like a cliff face from the poisoned earth.

We covered the final distance in minutes, the moat's stench hitting us long before we reached its edge. I pulled my tunic up over my nose, but it barely helped. The smell was overwhelming—rot and chemicals and death, a physical assault that made my eyes water. Adam slowed his bike, then stopped at the moat's edge. Clarence pulled up beside us.

We dismounted, our legs unsteady after such an unfamiliar action.

"We can't just leave them here," Adam said, looking at the bikes.

Clarence walked to the moat's edge, studying the thick, tar-like surface. "What if we..." He paused, then before anyone could stop him, he rolled his bike forward. It tipped over the edge and hit the moat's surface with a sound like a body falling into mud—wet, heavy, final. We watched in fascination as the bike was simply sucked beneath its surface. No splash. Nothing floated. The black surface swallowed it completely, closing over the machine like a mouth, leaving barely a ripple. Within seconds, there was no trace it had ever existed.

"Damn," I whispered.

Adam stared at the spot where the bike had vanished, then looked at his own motorcycle. "I guess that solves the problem."

He walked his bike to the edge and pushed it over. The same thing happened—the moat accepted it without protest, without sound, just absorbed the metal and rubber and fuel into its toxic depths as if adding one more piece of trash to a century's worth of accumulated poison.

But the stench was unbearable this close. I gagged, my body rebelling against the assault on my senses. The smell was more than just offensive—it was wrong on some fundamental level, like breathing in the essence of decay and corruption This was the Algorithm's legacy, I thought. The literal toxic waste of a system that consumed people and excreted their remains into a moat designed to keep everyone trapped.

The perfect symbol for the Undercity we'd escaped from. The perfect metaphor for the oligarchs' putrid souls, their rot disguised as order, their corruption hidden beneath the veneer of meritocracy. And we were volunteering to go right back into it.

I turned away from the moat, pressing my tunic harder against my face, trying not to vomit.

The bridge was in worse shape than we'd seen from a distance. Vines hung dead and brown, whole sections sagging toward the moat below. It looked like a strong wind might bring it down entirely.

I turned to Adam and Clarence not sure what we were going to do. "Do you see anyone?" I asked. "Any sign that Evelyn's been here?"

Adam shook his head, "No, I don't think she has. There would be tire tracks or foot prints. No one has been here before us recently."

"So either she hasn't arrived yet," Clarence said, "or she's waiting for us."

"Either way, we need decide if we're going over," Adam said. "The bridge won't hold forever. And those riders we left tied up will get free eventually, come looking for their bikes."

I looked at the bridge again, then at the city walls rising beyond it. Somewhere inside those walls, our people were hiding, waiting, hoping for rescue that might never come. Somewhere out there, Evelyn was executing her own plan, driven by hatred and ideology and the certainty that her way was right. And here we stood—three people with buried motorcycles, a hatchet, and determination that might not be enough to save anyone.

"Do we have any choice?" I asked

"There's really no turning back," Adam agreed. "We left that option behind when we dumped the bikes."

He was right. We could wait her for someone, the Rugis we beat up, Evelyn or some other band to find us. Or go forward—into the city, to the Ghosts, to whatever waited inside New Columbia's walls.

We all turned to look at what was left of the bridge. Several sections that had already fallen away, demonstrating just how fragile the structure had become. Enough to see that crossing it would most likely be suicide.

As if reading my mind Adam spoke the words that swirled in the back of my mind.

"Last chance to say no," he said, his voice muffled by the hand he'd pressed over his mouth and nose. "Once we get on that bridge, there won't be a way to return."

I looked at Clarence. He looked at me. Neither of us said anything.

"I'm going," I said.

"Me too," Clarence added.

Adam nodded slowly. "Then we go together."

Chapter 18

Blood for Blood

Hela led Evelyn to a motorcycle at dawn, gesturing to it with something that might have been amusement.

"This one's yours," Hela said. "Can you ride?"

Evelyn studied the machine. Crude construction, cobbled together from salvaged parts. The engine looked functional but primitive. Handlebars, clutch, gears—she understood the theory from technical manuals, from observing others. But theory and practice were different things.

"I have seen these units before," she said, keeping her voice level.

Hela's face was hard. "I didn't ask if you had seen one."

Around them, the Rugi camp was already stirring. Warriors emerged from their dwellings, checking weapons, preparing for the journey. Evelyn counted them—twelve riders total, including Hela. A full escort. Either Eraric was taking this mission seriously, or he wanted enough warriors present to kill her if she proved treacherous.

Probably both.

Evelyn approached the bike, running her hands over the controls. Clutch on the left handlebar. Throttle on the right. Gear shift by the left foot. Brake on the right. Simple enough in principle. She swung her leg over the seat, settling her weight. The bike tilted slightly under her, heavier than she expected and she had to catch it with her foot to prevent it falling over.

Behind her, she heard soft laughter from some of the younger warriors.

Evelyn's jaw tightened, but she ignored them. Focus on the machine. Focus on the task. Hela mounted her own bike with fluid grace, the motion so practiced it looked effortless. "Kick-start on the right side. Give it fuel with the throttle, then kick hard."

Evelyn found the kick-start, positioned her foot, and kicked.

Nothing.

"More throttle," Hela called. "And kick like you mean it."

Evelyn twisted the throttle slightly, feeling resistance, then kicked again. Harder this time.

The engine coughed, sputtered, then roared to life. The vibration ran through the entire frame, through her legs and up her spine. Loud. Powerful. Barely controlled. Evelyn glanced at Hela and thought she saw something. Something that looked like Hela was enjoying this a little too much.

"Good," Hela said, her voice carrying over the engine noise. "Now release the clutch slowly while giving it throttle. Ease into the gears."

Evelyn squeezed the clutch lever, shifted into first gear like she'd seen others do. Released the clutch.

Too fast.

The bike lurched forward violently. Evelyn's grip on the handlebars was the only thing that kept her from falling backward. The front wheel lifted slightly off the ground. She squeezed the clutch again in panic, and the bike stalled, dropping hard.

More laughter from the watching warriors.

Evelyn restarted the engine, her face hot with humiliation she refused to show. Years of ISB training, elite combat certification, tactical operations in the most dangerous parts of the Undercity—and she couldn't master a primitive motorcycle. She tried again. Released the clutch more slowly this time.

The bike moved forward in a jerky lurch, then stalled again. Again. And again.

On the fifth attempt, she got the clutch-throttle balance almost right. The bike lurched out from under her, shooting forward. Evelyn held on to the handle bars but her feet stayed on the ground causing her to be splayed out full body on the seat before she and the bike crashed to the ground.

The bike rolled over, nearly crushing her. She managed to get her leg out from under it, but the machine's weight pinned her partially, hot engine against her calf.

Hela dismounted, walking over with measured steps. She righted the bike with easy strength and waited for Evelyn to stand.

"Perhaps," Hela said quietly, though the entire camp could hear, "we might travel faster with you as a passenger."

The words landed like a physical blow. Evelyn was used to being in control. Leading. Now she was relegated to baggage class. That hurt worse than the burn on her calf now throbbing with pain.

"Fine," Evelyn said, the word tasting like ash in her mouth.

Hela gestured to one of her warriors—a broad-shouldered man named Garrick. "She rides with you. Keep her safe. She's valuable."

The last word carried weight. Not valuable as a person. Valuable as a tool. And only valuable as long as the tool was useful. She climbed onto the back of Garrick's bike, wrapping her arms around his waist, feeling the humiliation settle into her bones alongside the determination to never forget this moment.

Hela mounted her own bike again, scanning her assembled warriors. All engines were running now, filling the morning air with their collective rumble.

She revved her motor once, twice, then motioned them forward.

The group moved out in formation—Hela in the lead, other riders flanking and following, Evelyn trapped in the middle like cargo being transported.

They didn't follow the main road. Instead, Hela led them onto trails that wound through hills, cutting across terrain in ways that no proper road would follow. Shortcuts, Evelyn realized. Paths known only to those who'd traveled this land for generations.

The ride was immediately punishing. Within the first hour, Evelyn understood why Hela had smiled when mentioning the journey. The bike's suspension—if it could even be called that—transmitted every bump, every rock, every irregularity in the terrain directly through the seat into her spine.

Her arms ached from holding tight to Garrick's waist. Her legs burned from gripping the bike's sides for stability, not to mention the burning sensation leftover from the engine burn. Her entire body jarred and jolted with each rough patch of trail. And they'd barely begun.

The sun climbed higher as they rode. The landscape shifted from forest to hills, from hills to wide flat plains, from plains back to rougher terrain. Always heading north. Always at the maximum speed the crude bikes could manage. Which wasn't fast. Maybe forty kilometers per hour on smooth sections. Less on rough ground. The engines whined and roared, working hard, generating heat. Evelyn's extra weight, while not excessive, caused the bike to react sluggishly, which frustrated the driver exceedingly.

After what felt like an eternity but was probably only ninety minutes, Hela raised her hand and slowed. The group came to a stop in a clearing.

"Cooling break," she announced. "Three minutes. Stretch. Drink. Don't wander."

Evelyn dismounted, her legs weak when they took her full weight. She was aware of every muscle from her inner thighs gripping the bike to her hands cramped into claws from holding on. She forced herself to stand straight, to walk normally, to show no weakness despite the pain.

Around her, the Rugi warriors dismounted with easy familiarity, stretching casually, passing water skins, chatting like this was a pleasant morning ride rather than a brutal cross-country journey. Hela approached, studying Evelyn's face. "How are you holding up?"

"Fine," Evelyn said.

"Liar." Hela's smile was cold. "But a proud liar. I respect that." She gestured to the bikes. "We have eleven more hours of this. Maybe twelve, depending on terrain. The route through the hills is rough. Saves distance but not as smooth of a ride."

"Why not take the main road?" Evelyn asked. "If it is faster."

"Its not." Hela's eyes glinted. "The main road is longer. We might travel faster but the total time is the same. Besides its patrolled. We'd be visible for kilometers. This way, we arrive unseen in a position to watch for your companions when they approach the bridge."

"Mount up," Hela called to her warriors. "We move in one minute."

The pattern repeated. Ninety minutes of brutal riding, three minutes to cool the engines, then back on the bikes. The sun tracked across the sky. The landscape blurred into a continuous stream of pain and vibration and burning muscles. By the fourth stop, Evelyn's hands were cramping from gripping Garrick's leather armor. By the sixth, she could barely feel her legs. By the eighth, she was existing in a state somewhere between consciousness and dissociation, her mind retreating from her body's screaming protests.

The Rugi warriors showed no such struggle. They rode with the ease of people who'd been doing this their entire lives, for whom motorcycles were as natural as walking. Afternoon stretched into evening. The sun began its descent toward the western horizon, painting the plains in shades of amber and gold.

"Are we getting close?" Evelyn asked during one of the cooling breaks, her voice hoarse from breathing exhaust and dust all day.

Hela consulted with one of her scouts, then turned back. "Three more hours. Maybe four. We'll make camp before full darkness, rest, then approach the city at dawn."

Three more hours. Evelyn's body rebelled at the thought, but her will was stronger than her body. It always had been. They rode on as twilight descended, the bikes' headlights cutting through gathering darkness, following trails that were barely visible even in daylight. Finally, as the last light faded from the sky, Hela signaled a halt.

They'd stopped in a depression surrounded by low hills—defensible position, hidden from casual observation, with good sight lines in all directions. The warriors dismounted and began making camp with practiced efficiency. No fires—smoke would be visible for kilometers. Just cold food, water, and the bikes arranged in a defensive perimeter. Evelyn lowered herself from Garrick's bike and immediately collapsed.

Her legs simply gave out, cramping violently. She hit the ground hard, unable to catch herself, her hands too stiff to break her fall properly. Hela walked to her slowly, enjoying seeing her weakness, pulling Evelyn to her feet. "Walk it off. The cramps will pass faster if you move."

Evelyn stood and stretched, remembering her training. She paced, each step agony, muscles locked and burning. Slowly, painfully, the cramps began to ease.

"I thought we had trained for everything," Evelyn said when she could speak without gasping. "But nothing trained me for this. That kicked my butt. Literally."

Hela's laugh was genuine, surprised. "Welcome to Rugi life. We're born on these machines. Learn to ride before we can walk properly. Even our children could manage what you just survived."

"That's supposed to make me feel better?"

"No. It should make you more ashamed." Hela handed her a water skin. "You're not Rugi. You may be top warrior in your prison, but here you can't compete with a simple Rugi child much less a warrior. It's good to see how easily the demon in you can be broken."

Hela stood, puffed chest, eyes glowing.

Evelyn ignored the insults. She drank deeply, the water sharp and cold and perfect. "How far did we cover?"

"Maybe four hundred kilometers. Maybe four-fifty." Hela stood with hands at back, legs spread in parade rest. Evelyn couldn't help but notice how comfortable she appeared despite the same journey that had nearly destroyed Evelyn.

"We're within striking distance of the city now. Twenty kilometers, maybe twenty-five. Close enough to see the walls at sunrise."

"What is your plan?"

"We make ourselves visible," Hela said. "Ride out onto the plains where anyone approaching the bridge will see us coming. I want to draw your companions' attention. Make them hesitate."

"They have nowhere to flee, they'll rush the bridge."

"Exactly. I sent a scout ahead earlier—he's watching for them on the road. When they pass, he'll come back to let us they are close. We'll position ourselves between them and the bridge, make ourselves obvious. They'll have to decide whether to cross the bridge or run."

"They'll run," Evelyn said with certainty. "Adam won't let anything stop him from trying to reach those walls."

"Good. Then we'll have a nice dance with them." Hela's expression hardened. "We get to deal with escaped demons in a way that will send a message to the others not try to enter Kuhtara." Hela turned to face Evelyn eye to eye. "We'll be sure you get inside. Just know this, if you fail and return to us, I will personally run my blade through your heart. You are not welcome here, devil, and once my word is fulfilled to deliver you to your tunnel, I will make certain you never return, dead or alive."

Evelyn grinned. "Spoken like a true warrior. I salute your honor, and vow the very same to you."

The two shared a moment of eye contact. The moment was brief, but both felt a sense of esprit before

Hela continued "The waste pipe entrance is on the south side of the walls, hidden by a drainage ditch. The pipe itself runs maybe twenty meters under the moat before reaching the grate. You'll need to wade through…" She paused, searching for words.

"I know what waste pipes contain," Evelyn said. "I've operated in the Undercity. I know filth."

"Not like this. This is a hundred fold worse than you can imagine. Not just the accumulated sewage from a city of a quarter million people." Hela met her eyes. "You'll be crawling through a toxic sludge that would make most warriors lose their lunch in an instant. Through darkness and rot and death. Are you sure you're strong enough, tender-ass?"

Evelyn smiled and rubbed her backside. "Yes."

"You mentioned you have a blood-debt to pay. What is it that waits for you?"

"The man who betrayed me, who destroyed my career, who threw me away like garbage—he's inside those walls. He thinks he is untouchable, protected by layers of power. He thought he could simply toss me to the lions without consequence."

"And you're going to prove him wrong."

"I'm going to be his consequence."

Hela nodded slowly. "When I became a warrior I swore the same oath. Blood for blood. Justice through payment."

"We're not so different," Evelyn observed.

"No," Hela agreed. "We aren't. I admit that I have seen reflections of myself in you. I respect the warrior in you." She stepped forward offering her hand. "Rest.

We rise before dawn. By this time tomorrow, you'll either be inside your city, or dead in that pipe."

Evelyn took the offered hand, letting Hela pull her to her feet. "I won't die in a sewer."

"No," Hela said, studying her face. "I don't think you will."

The camp settled into quiet as darkness deepened. Warriors took watch positions while others rested. Evelyn found a patch of ground slightly elevated from the rest, wrapped herself in the blanket Hela provided, and tried to let exhaustion pull her into sleep. But even as tired as she was, sleep came slowly.

Tomorrow she'd reach New Columbia. Tomorrow she'd crawl through filth and darkness to get inside. Tomorrow she'd begin hunting Julius Locke through the Undercity's passages. Tomorrow everything would change.

She stared up at the stars—more visible here than anywhere in New Columbia, where light pollution had blocked all but the brightest—and allowed herself a small smile. The Rugi thought they were using her. Eraric thought he was protecting his territory.

They were all correct, in their way. But they were also all tools, serving Evelyn's larger purpose without realizing it. By the time they understood what she really was, what she really wanted, it would be too late.

The Algorithm's values would spread here. Order would be imposed. The Keeper's weak cooperation would crumble under the weight of proper hierarchy and competition. And the lawless society of outlaw tribes would be hunted down and exterminated.

Evelyn closed her eyes and let exhaustion finally claim her. Tomorrow. Tomorrow it all began.

Chapter 19

Interception

The scout appeared on the ridge like a spirit materialized from dust, his bike kicking up a thin trail as he crested the hill. Hela watched him approach, reading his body language before he even reached their camp. The way he sat forward on the machine, the urgency in his throttle control—he'd found something.

She raised her fist. Behind her, the column of twelve riders slowed, engines dropping to idle. Evelyn sat behind Garrick three bikes back, her posture rigid despite the hours of punishment. The woman had surprised Hela. She was obviously suffering. Saddle sore and weary, but just as a Rugi warrior would do, she did not complain, or whimper. It was obvious she fought to show the pain. Respectable, even for a demon from the inside the walls.

The scout pulled alongside, killing his motor. Dust settled around them.

"Commander." He kept his voice low, though the plains stretched empty in all directions. Old habit. Good habit. "The devils. On the road north, maybe eight kilometers out. Three of them."

Hela's hand moved to the knife at her belt, fingers brushing the worn leather handle. "On foot?"

"Bikes." The scout's expression darkened. "Our

bikes. Tarek and Merin's machines."

Behind her, someone cursed. Hela felt the anger ripple through her riders like heat off stone. Two of their brothers assigned to road-kill patrol as they referred to scavenging off transports they had disabled. Now these demons rode their machines.

"They must have killed Tarek and Merin," Wexar said, his voice hard, "how else would they have the bikes?"

Hela nodded, recognizing the truth. The demons couldn't have taken bikes from warriors without bloodshed. No Rugi would forfeit their bike without a fight to the death. "What more did you see?" She demanded.

"They're moving fast," the scout continued. "Pushing the machines hard, should reach the bridge within the hour."

Hela calculated distances, timing, approach angles. The bridge lay almost directly west of their current position, perhaps fifteen kilometers across open ground. If they rode hard, they could cut the angle, reach the southern approach before the demons arrived from the north. She glanced back at Evelyn. The woman met her eyes, face unreadable despite obvious exhaustion.

"You promised them to me," Hela said. Not a question.

"I promised them to you," Evelyn confirmed.

She motioned for Garrick to bring her closer.

"These are your people, tell me what to expect from them, what plans have they laid out?"

Evelyn thought about them killing two warriors, stealing their bikes. It honestly shocked her. She never dreamed that they would have had it in them to fight.

"Until this moment, I would have told you they were cowards and not to worry. But the fact that they bested two of your warriors; given that they are just an old man, a boy and a civilian woman…"

Evelyn let the point sink a minute remembering Hela's chiding her about not being able to ride. It was Hela's turn to ignore the question.

"Will they stand and fight, or will they run?"

"They will hide, bait you into striking, and attack from another position you didn't expect. Do not trust them to fight fair."

"What will they expect?"

"They'll expect me to be leading. Its me they have come to stop. You will be able to drive them up onto the bridge, because they will try to defend the opening. Once you have them pushed onto the bridge, they will have no place to go. Inside, my enforcers have undoubtedly fortified the opening against intruders. You will be able to pick them off at your leisure."

Hela liked that answer.

"Mount up," she commanded.

The column came alive. Engines roared. Hela swung onto her bike, feeling the familiar weight settle beneath her. She looked at the scout. "Lead. Fast as you can. We take the direct route."

They moved as one, twelve machines cutting across the plains like a blade through flesh. The trail Hela had been following—the safer path, the one that used the land's contours for concealment—no longer mattered. Speed mattered. Interception mattered. She opened her throttle and felt the wind tear at her face, hot and dry and carrying the taste of distant smoke.

The land blurred past. Hela's world narrowed to the machine beneath her, the vibration running through her bones, the endless expanse of yellow grass and sage breaking before them. Her riders maintained formation without signals—years of training, hunting, warfare had taught them to move like water flowing downhill. Fluid. Inevitable.

Twenty minutes of hard riding brought them within sight of the bridge.

It rose from the plains like something diseased. Hela had seen it from a distance before, during reconnaissance runs over the past months. But never this close. Never with intention to approach. The structure arched across the black waters of the moat, a tangle of dead and dying vegetation that seemed to writhe even in stillness. Vines thick as her thigh, now gray and rotting. Flowers that had blazed red and gold, according to the scouts' reports, now reduced to brown husks.

The bridge was dying. The prison-city was killing it.

"There." Wexar pointed.

North of the bridge, movement. Three figures on bikes, still distant but closing. Hela raised the spyglass she'd liberated from a dead Kuhtaran scout ten years ago—back when she'd been young and foolish enough to believe the Keeper's servants could be reasoned with. She focused the lens.

Three demons. Two men, one woman. The lead rider—older, scarred face, warrior's bearing despite city-clothes—that would be their leader. The one Evelyn had called Adam. The second man was thinner, nervous, riding with the uncertain balance of someone unused to machines. The woman rode behind the leader, pressed close, her hair whipping in the wind.

They were pushing the bikes hard. Too hard. One of the machines coughed black smoke from its exhaust, the engine clearly damaged.

Hela lowered the spyglass and handed it to Evelyn.

Evelyn took it, raising it to her eye with practiced efficiency. For a moment she was silent, studying the approaching riders. Then she lowered the glass, her face carefully blank.

"Promise delivered," Evelyn said quietly.

Hela looked at the bridge again, this time truly studying it. The structure sagged in the middle, whole sections visibly rotten. The demons would have to cross it. Would have to trust their weight to that decaying mass of vegetable matter. She did the calculation automatically—three people, maybe two hundred kilograms total. The bridge might hold. Or it might collapse and send them into the black waters below.

"We either slaughter them ourselves," Hela said, half to herself, "or they sink into the hell of putrid waters. Whichever the gods desire, Kuhtara will be rid of the demons that escaped." She turned to look at Evelyn. "Except for one, which we'll dispatch now."

Evelyn met her gaze without flinching. "Our agreement."

"Yes." Hela gestured toward the moat. "Your agreement."

She guided her bike forward, moving slowly now, approaching the southern edge where the moat curved closest to the plains. The stench hit first—chemical and organic rot combined, a smell that made her eyes water and throat close. The black waters barely moved, thick as tar, swallowing light.

"There." Hela pointed. "See the pipe?"

Evelyn followed her gesture. The waste pipe emerged from the base of the prison-city's wall, cutting across the moat like a metal bridge. It was perhaps three meters in diameter, corroded steel mottled with rust and mineral deposits. The top section rose above the moat's surface—two meters exposed, one meter submerged. At the far end, where the pipe met the wall, Hela could see the welded steel grate that sealed the entrance.

"The grate's welded shut," Hela explained, "but there's a break on the south side. Big enough to climb through if you're determined. The pipe runs maybe twenty meters before it reaches the internal conduit system. From there..." She shrugged. "You're in the belly of your prison-city. Where exactly, I don't know. No Rugi has ever been fool enough to crawl through demon filth."

Evelyn dismounted and moved to the moat's edge, studying the pipe with tactical precision. Hela watched her calculate angles, distances, risks. The woman was a warrior, no question. Misguided perhaps, serving demons rather than gods, but a warrior nonetheless.

They stood in silence for a moment, two warriors on opposite sides of an ancient divide, united only by temporary alliance and mutual contempt. Hela thought about the journey here, Evelyn's stubborn endurance, her refusal to show weakness even when her body was clearly failing. In another world, another life, they might have been shield-sisters. In this world, they were tools using each other.

Hela extended her forearm, the warrior's farewell. Evelyn gripped it, their hands clasping just below the elbow.

"No love between us," Hela said.

"No love," Evelyn agreed. "Only respect."

"Respect." Hela released her grip. "When you reach your demon city, remember this: the Rugi will never accept the Keeper's chaos. Your people staying locked behind those walls is the only thing preventing war. If you or demons return, we will hunt them. Every single one of you."

"Then we understand each other perfectly."

Hela turned back to look at the base of the bridge. She could see them now without the spyglass—three figures. She watched in anger as the demons pushed the bikes into the black death of the moat.

"Another reason to hate them," she muttered to herself.

Chapter 20

Bissu Seated

Lee had been awake for a while. Not fully moving—just lying there, eyes open, listening to Petrahn breathe itself into morning. The city had a rhythm now, one they were starting to recognize: distant footfalls on stone, the low hum of wind moving through terraces, the faint murmur of voices rising with the light. It should have been calming. It wasn't.

Adam, Iris, and Clarence with the shared understanding that this might be the last time. Lee had watched the van disappear into the open plain and told themselves what they always did before an operation.

If you don't imagine the ending, it can't hurt you. They swung their legs off the sleeping platform and stood, restless. The council had been clear: if the Ghosts succeeded, Petrahn would change overnight. Refugees from New Columbia—people shaped by fear, scarcity, and score keeping—would pour into a world that had never measured human worth in numbers. Lee was meant to help with that. To stand between cultures. To translate. Assuming there was anyone left to translate for.

How exactly they were supposed to do that was the big mystery.

They were reaching for their boots when Alo

stepped into the doorway.

Lee knew Alo well enough by now to recognize the difference. When Alo was casual, she leaned. When she was curious, she tilted her head. When something was wrong—she stood very still.

"The council has requested your presence," Alo said.

Lee didn't answer right away. Their chest tightened—not panic, not yet—but the cold compression of a trained mind recognizing a bad pattern.

"Did they say why? Are Adam and the others OK?" Lee asked.

"They did not say."

That was answer enough. Lee pulled on their tunic, movements efficient, controlled. "Lead the way."

The corridors felt longer than usual. The light sharper. Lee kept their breathing steady, refusing to let their thoughts race ahead of the facts. Soldiers didn't panic before the reports were given. They waited for confirmation.

The Council Hall doors were already open. The elders were assembled. Tahoma at the center. Nyamba's seat empty, as expected—but it still struck Lee harder than it should have. Tahoma inclined his head.

"Lee. Thank you for coming so promptly."

"You have news from Adam?" Lee asked flatly.

A ripple moved through the council—not surprise, but recognition. There was no point pretending with them. Tahoma folded his hands. "No. Not as far as we know."

Lee didn't relax. Not yet.

"We do know that the van was struck by a Rugian roadside bomb yesterday on the road to city," Tahoma continued. "The driver reported no injuries. The Ghosts abandoned the vehicle and were last seen moving on foot toward New Columbia."

Lee let out a breath they hadn't realized they were holding.

"Of course they did," they said. "Walking into hell like it's just another bad neighborhood."

Alo's voice came quietly from behind them. "They were not pursued."

"Yet," Lee muttered.

"There is another matter," Tahoma said, and this time the weight in his voice was different—not grim, but deliberate. "One that concerns the days ahead."

Lee turned back, attentive.

"As you realize, when the gates open," Tahoma continued, "Petrahn will change. Kuhtara will change. We will be asking people who have lived under surveillance, hierarchy, and enforced scarcity to suddenly exist in a culture built on trust and shared responsibility."

Lee nodded. "That kind of shock doesn't fade quietly."

"No," Tahoma agreed. "It fractures. And fractured minds seek voices."

One of the other councilors leaned forward. "We have mediated conflict among Kuhtarans for generations. But this—" he paused, choosing his words carefully, "—this will not be a single people in disagreement. It will be two histories colliding."

"Some will see the city dwellers as rigid," another added. "Others will see Kuhtarans as disordered. Weak."

Lee exhaled through their nose. "And New Colombians will carry their own hierarchies with them. Old grievances. Old scores."

Tahoma inclined his head. "Exactly. We cannot be seen as impartial arbiters in those conflicts. We don't yet understand what those grievances might be? Resources, food issues, changes in a way of life that feels different can cause stress. We need to be able to answer questions knowledgeably in order to arrive at the best conclusion. In order to assist them, we must know *how* to assist them."

Silence stretched—not uncomfortable, but expectant.

"We are asking you," Tahoma said at last, "to consider joining the council."

Lee blinked.

Not disbelief—calculation.

"You will be the presence New Colombians will recognize as one of their own."

A murmur of assent moved around the chamber.

"You understand their wounds," Sani added. "Their instincts. Their fears. And you have already shown that you can stand between worlds without trying to dominate either."

Lee's jaw tightened—not from resistance, but from the sudden gravity of it.

Tahoma's gaze softened. "The Keeper identified

you almost immediately upon your arrival. Before we did. She saw that you were… resonant," Tahoma continued. "Someone shaped by contradiction rather than broken by it."

Lee felt their cheeks flush.

"Nyamba, you told me the role of Bissu was to help people cross thresholds," they said slowly. "Between selves. Between stories. Between ways of living." A faint, incredulous breath escaped them. "I didn't realize you meant this."

"This is not a command," Nyamba said gently. "It is an invitation for you to choose. It is the Kuhtaran way."

Lee looked around the hall. At the stone. The light. The quiet weight of people who understood what they were asking.

"I'm honored," Lee said at last, and they meant it fully. "Truly. I just—" they shook their head once, a small, self-aware smile flickering across their face, "—never imagined the Undercity would prepare me for a seat like this."

"It prepared you precisely for this," Tahoma replied.

The council waited.

Lee did not answer yet, thinking about their own journey—how terrifying it had been to step through that door, to cross the bridge into an unknown world. How even now, surrounded by abundance and kindness, part of them still waited for the trap to spring, for the measurement to begin, for someone to decide they weren't worthy.

"Thousands will come," Sani continued. "Thousands who have been waiting their entire lives for a door to open. Who have been dying slowly under the Algorithm's calculations. Who will risk everything for the chance at something better."

"Believe me, I know all too well what they will be feeling. I'm still going through it, you know," Lee repeated numbly.

Nyamba leaned forward, her face serious. "This mass migration may pose serious conflicts and disagreements for many of the people of Kuhtara, because they will be fearful. The Algorithm's values are infectious, Lee. They spread. They corrupt. We've worked for a century to build a world based on cooperation, on abundance, on freedom. And now we're about to invite in thousands of people trained to compete, to take things by force or coercion, who want to impose hierarchy on a society built on equity This council will have to respond to those types of questions, which we admit, are new to us."

"You need someone on the Council who can speak for them," Lee said, understanding crystallizing. "Someone who came from inside. Someone who can vouch that they're not... not evil. Just conditioned."

"Exactly," Tahoma said. "We have the resources to receive them. The Keeper has already begun preparing infrastructures. Food, housing, medical care—all of that is manageable. But the psychological integration? The cultural bridge? That's where we'll either succeed or watch everything collapse into conflict."

Lee looked at Tahoma, then to the rest of the

council. "All of this presumes success on getting in and out of New Columbia."

"She has calculated probabilities," Tahoma confessed. "But Lee—she cannot predict human choice. She can only create opportunities and hope that humans choose wisely."

The Council members nodded in agreement. Lee considered each of them in turn—Nyamba's weathered wisdom, Tahoma's quiet strength, Sani's practical efficiency, Arwen's gentle confidence. These were people who had spent decades serving their community, who had earned their positions through years of experience and learning.

And they were asking Lee—barely an adult by New Columbia's standards, still carrying trauma like an open wound—to sit among them.

"I'm younger than everyone here," Lee said evenly. "Decades younger. And when the people from New Columbia arrive, they'll see a council of eight Kuhtarans and one city-born Bissu." A small tilt of the head. "That won't read as neutral to them. It will look… stacked."

The chamber did not respond all at once.

Instead, a low murmur moved through the council—uncoordinated, overlapping, unguarded.

Lee caught fragments.

"You see? This is exactly why the Keeper called them to us."

"The question of impartiality—honestly, it would never have crossed my mind."

"No, no, it's cultural. They think judgment is

being rendered."

"Do they believe they're on trial?"

"But it isn't a competition between contestants—"

"Foreign way of thinking. Entirely foreign."

Lee remained still, listening, surprised by the absence of defensiveness. No one contradicted her. No one corrected her framing. They were not weighing her worth—they were weighing the problem.

The murmuring gradually softened. The council did not rush to consensus; it allowed itself to arrive.

Tahoma rose slightly from his seat—not to conclude, but to respond.

"This," he said, gesturing gently toward Lee, "is precisely the kind of question we need to be asking."

He looked around the circle. "We speak often of non-judgment. Of guidance rather than verdict. Yet we did not initially see how our own structure might appear through the lens of the city."

His gaze returned to Lee. "The choice is yours to refuse or accept the call. We are not trying to convince you to accept it. We are doing what we do."

"Mediating," Anwen added.

Tahoma nodded. "You have helped identify a situational concern. In doing so, you have already begun the work."

He let the implication settle.

"You will teach us how the council appears to those raised under the Algorithm. How fairness is expected to look. And we will teach you how to help them understand how justice functions here—not as a balance of power, but as a shared responsibility."

Lee felt something shift—not relief, not certainty, but alignment.

"So," Tahoma continued, "when the arrivals question the council's makeup, you will name the concern openly. Not to defend us. Not to override them. But to help them understand that this is not a trial, not a contest, not a metric."

A pause.

"And when we miss something shaped by city-thinking," Anwen said, "you will help us understand as well."

"Sheesh," Lee said letting out a full breath. "Do you guys ever ask *easy* questions?"

Chapter 21

Burning Bridge

The question of Evelyn hung between us as we reached the base of the bridge, unspoken but heavy enough that I could feel it pressing against my ribs.

"What about Evelyn?" I asked finally. "Are we sure she'll come here."

Adam swatted the gnats away from his face. Swirls of the nasty biting flies the only sign of life along the edges of the black death we were standing next to. "We are," he said confidently. "There's only one way in, and you know she'll try to keep us out. I'm sure that by now she realizes the bridge is failing too."

The bridge loomed above us, and we could hear stress fractures and tendrils snapping as the vines slowly succumbed to the massive weight they were supporting.

Clarence glanced up and grimaced. "Calling that thing 'failing' feels optimistic."

"If Evelyn reaches it after us," Adam went on, "she'll follow us straight into the city. It's our duty to stop her."

"And your solution," I said carefully, already knowing the answer, "is to destroy it."

"Yeah, as we cross," he said.

"Why make that decision now?" I said. "Why trap ourselves with no way out. If we get to the other side and its closed, are you willing to just give up that easily?"

Adam stared at me, considering the facts. "You still don't have to do this. But I'm counting on the fact that if the bridge hasn't fallen, the door is open. What's inside I can't say, but if we get to the door, there won't be time to go back and sabotage the bridge. The best we can hope is to seal the door from inside. Again, an unknown. So, I'll ask again, are you coming?

I nodded my head. The answer had settled in me long before he asked. "I'm coming."

He held my gaze a moment longer, searching for hesitation, for fear. There was fear—of course there was—but in that moment, I knew there was no other option.

"Hold on to your hats, folks." Clarence said, looking across the plains. A thin brown smear was rising on the horizon, widening by the second. Dust. Too much of it to be weather. Too fast to be animals.

"Motorcycles," he said. "Rugian. A dozen, maybe more."

They were coming hard, engines faint but unmistakable now, bearing straight for the bridge.

He looked back at us, expression calm in that unsettling way he had when the math had already finished running.

"Well," he said matter-of-factly, "that answers that. Shall we go?"

Adam looked at each of us once. No debate left to have. He nodded, short and final, then shifted his weight forward onto the bridge.

The bridge groaned under his weight. He stopped and waited to listen to signs of breaking. What we heard was a low fibrous sigh, like the sound of a breath pulled through a throat that was closing. The vines responded to his weight with a slow adjustment, cords tightening where they could, becoming loose where they could not.

The bridge dipped. Only a few inches, but enough. The motion traveled outward in a delayed wave, the tendrils shuddering one after another, out of sync. A fine dust lifted from the surface—dry rot, powdered bark—catching the light before falling into the moat and disappearing without a trace.

The rotting smell of the bridge reached me then. Not rot exactly. Something mineral and sour beneath it, like wet grass sealed too long from air.

Adam began working his way up to the top of the bridge platform. Clarence came next. Carefully pulling at vines, testing his weight on them. When he finally pulled himself up to the flat surface of the bridge, another sound followed, closer now. A faint tearing, cloth pulled too far. One of the outer cords near the anchoring edge split lengthwise, not breaking free, just opening. The gap widened slowly, exposing a pale, fibrous interior that should not have been visible.

Clarence tightened his grip on the strap of his pack. No one spoke. He eased his full weight onto the bridge. It held.

Barely.

I pulled myself up onto the bridge behind the two men. The surface rolled under me as soon as my weight transferred, a slow lateral sway that forced my breath out through my teeth. Clarence looked back holding tightly as the bridge shifted under my weight. Then we all began to move, careful, deliberate.

I could feel the vines compress, then slid against one another. When we first crossed, the bridge had carried us without hesitation. It had risen to meet our steps. The surface had been warm, almost buoyant, the tendrils thick and green, the blossoms bright enough to hurt my eyes. We'd run. The structure had taken the impact and given nothing back but speed. It had felt permanent then. Assured. As if it had always been there and always would be.

Now it felt aware of every gram.

I flattened myself further, chest against the vines, spreading my weight over a larger surface area,pulling and sliding myself forward. Each movement sent a tremor ahead of us, a delayed response that rippled down the length of the span.

The far side felt impossibly distant. One hundred meters had never been far before. Now it stretched. Each meter claimed individually. I could feel the bridge sagging more toward the center, the arc deepening beneath our combined weight. Gravity was patient. It did not need to hurry.

Adam paused once, hand raised, and we froze where we were. The bridge continued to move after we stopped, a slow settling that made my stomach tighten. Somewhere below us, a strand gave way. I didn't hear it break free. I felt the loss, a subtle drop, a redistribution that traveled through the structure and into my ribs.

Clarence was a few feet ahead of me, stretched flat against the bridge, moving by inches. His elbows dug in, his boots searching for purchase in the woven mass beneath him. The bridge dipped under his weight, then dipped again.

Then the surface gave way. A sudden gaping hole appeared below Clarence's legs. Clarence dropped with it. His hands grasped tight around the remaining weave as the section of the bridge beneath his hips tore free. His legs vanished through the opening, dangling into open air. I heard the sound of falling debris slapping the black moat below and watched as it fell, like slow motion, into the sticky stinking tar. The surface barely rippled as fragments of vine and leaf drifted down, striking the surface once before being swallowed. The muck closed over them without a sound.

I flattened myself even more, gripping the fragments of vine tightly, feeling the structure bounce and sway as Clarence pulled himself back up. He dragged one knee onto the deck, then the other, breathing hard, smeared with damp green pulp and black rot. He didn't look back. I didn't blame him.

I edged forward to the torn section. The bridge was no longer a smooth secure structure, but a mass of uncertainty and failing parts. As I edged myself along the thicker edges around the hole that Clarence had just escaped, I prayed it would continue to hold us just long enough to give us passage to the wall.

The wall! I suddenly remembered. I strained to

see ahead if the door still remained open. The sway of the bridge pulled my thoughts forward and backward at once. My eyes strained to where the far end should meet the wall, but the vines there had grown thick, curling over the opening, obscuring it from view. I swallowed against the sudden tightness in my throat.

What if it wasn't there now? What if the Keeper— or the Enforcers—had closed, sealing the path, leaving us suspended above the black moat with no way through?

I remembered that first crossing, the dust and grit of the tunnel, the clang of metal as we forced the barrier open. That moment had felt almost sacred— danger and possibility intertwined. The opening had suddenly been discovered, and luckily it had yielded to us. And now, as I hung a dozen meters above the tar, the memory sharpened the fear in my chest: what if this time it would not yield?

My mind raced as I remembered being chased. What if the Enforcers had discovered it and sealed it? Nyamba and the council had said the Keeper had anticipated our coming, it had decided to guard itself again, closing its veins against us returning to it?

My fingers gripped the vine, boots seeking purchase on the trembling bridge. Every sway of the living weave made my stomach churn. The bridge itself sounded like it was reacting to my fears, aware of my hesitation, creaking and sighing under our weight, the sound echoing the pulse of my own fear. Inch by inch, we moved forward, but the memory and the possibility of the doorway's disappearance pressed down on me as heavily as the black water waiting far below.

As we reached the center of the bridge, Adam had perched near the edge on one side, motioning for us to come on ahead of him. He pointed to the huge gaping hole where a large portion had given way, leaving only the two outer strands of the vines holding the bridge together.

"Stay on the outer edge of the bridge," he said, "where it's thicker and stronger than the bridge deck. The center of the bridge is its weakest point, we should be OK after we get past this part."

I pointed at the vine covered end at the wall. "The door is covered by vines." I said. "That is, if the door is still there."

Adam looked past me, in the opposite direction, his eyes squinting into the sunlight.

"I sure hope so, because were about to get company."

I looked back to what he was looking at. The Rugi were now approaching the road where the van had been waiting for us a short distance from the end of the bridge.

Evelyn was not with them.

Adam called over to Clarence.

"You and Iris get up to the wall and start clearing those vines. I am going to give the Rugi a little obstacle to overcome."

He began climbing back the way we had come, to the point where Clarence had broke through. He pulled off the pack on his back and pulled out a hatchet and began chopping through the rotting timbers.

Clarence didn't hesitate and pulled himself across the wider opening that now faced us and began to scramble towards the other end. I followed.

It didn't take long for Adam to make quick work of that end of the bridge, but it didn't fall. The separate section still stood, but was no longer connected to what we were climbing. We continued to claw our way along the edge of the swaying structure as Adam started back up toward us. He was just past the second open section when the Rugi reached the base of the bridge. They did not waste time checking to see if the bridge was sound, suddenly rushing up with their knives drawn.

The first four Rugi to reach the bridge did not hesitate, immediately rushing forward. They sprinted with knives in hand, aiming to catch us before we reached the far side. Their section of the bridge shivered beneath them, responding to the sudden weight. Then the section Adam had severed a few minutes earlier shuddered violently and collapsed, sending them tumbling into the moat along with fragments of vines and debris.

The muck bubbled and sucked at them, thick and unrelenting. Three clawed desperately at the edges, pulling themselves back onto the ruined bridge, coughing and sputtering. The fourth sank beneath the stinking surface, leaving only a trail of dark ripples behind. The remaining Rugi scrambled to regroup at the edge of the moat, now separated from us by the gaping distance of the missing bridge.

I inched forward, knees and forearms pressed to the deck, heart hammering, praying the outer strands held. We were completely cut off from retreat. I felt the fear settle in—I wondered if I would die on this bridge over a river that smelled of human filth.

Adam was crouched near the second broken section, hatchet clutched in anticipation of making a second opening when he saw the bridge portion collapse. As Clarence and I pressed on towards the wall still about twenty-five meters away, Adam scrambled to quickly catch up with us.

The air seemed to thrum, vibrating along the bridge as we pushed the limits of its fragility. I had watched how quickly the Rugi had slipped below the surface of the tarry waters below and suddenly knew our fate should the rest of the bridge gave way.

Then came the first arrow, flaming at the tip, hurtling from across the moat. It struck the center of the bridge with a dull thud, fire immediately shot up along the dry, brittle vines. The flames hungrily devoured the sections Adam had weakened, but the wetter, rotting areas slowed its progress, smoldering instead of sending the entire bridge into immediate inferno.

"Keep low! And keep moving" Adam yelled.

I flattened myself, boots searching for purchase, forearms dragging across the trembling weave, every sense alert. Clarence had made the wall ahead, hacking and pulling at the vines over the doorway, looking for a space for us to slip through. I kept crawling toward him, each inch closer felt like hanging on a silk thread above the abyss.

The second arrow struck, then a third. Sparks showered around us, and the smoke thickened, curling in dark ribbons. My lungs burned as I crawled forward, each movement measured, deliberate. The bridge bounced beneath our combined weight, moaning like a beast in pain, but it held.

I could see the Rugi at the far side, retreating but still shouting, their knives glinting, their eyes wild. The end of the bridge near Adam's severed section swung slightly in the wind, a reminder that there was no way back for us.

The vines of the doorway, thick and tightly woven, clung stubbornly to the wall, resisting Clarence's attempts to free them. Adam joined with his own hatchet, chopping at what seemed to be the last living vines on the bridge, tough and stringy fibers refusing to give way under our onslaught.

Behind us, the bridge crackled with fire. The Rugi had slowed their urgency realizing there was no escape for us. They were now sending lazy shots into the bridge in long lobs clearly enjoying the idea of our death by fire.

Each chop of the ax rang like the tolling of a bell, the smoke from the fires threatening to choke us before the flames could reach us.

Chapter 22

Underworld

Evelyn reached the wastewater conduit as the sound of the Rugian bikes roared into the distance. The pipe ended in a steel grate welded to rebar embedded in concrete. Evelyn braced herself against the curve of the conduit and leaned forward, peering through the bars. They were fused with age and mineral bloom, thick enough that even the water had long since given up trying to pass through. She struck the grate once with the butt of her knife to test for weakness. The sound went nowhere, swallowed by the awful black waste pooled behind it.

Evelyn's ISB training had taught her to compartmentalize sensory input during operations. Pain could be set aside. Fear could be managed. Disgust was just another signal to be acknowledged and ignored. She focused on the task: find the break, get through, reach the Undercity.

She shifted along one edge of the conduit, boots sinking into the black slurry with each step. The surface gave reluctantly, clinging, dragging at her as she moved. The waste reached her thighs, then her waist, warm and heavy, breathing out a stench that coated the back of her throat. She forced down the reflex to gag and continued probing the wall with her free hand, fingers sliding over slick stone, seams long ago calcified shut. No opening.

She pushed deeper. The ooze rose to her chest, pressure tightening around her ribs. One hand stayed high on the wall while the other searched—feeling for weakness, for a break, for the promise Hela had pointed out with such certainty. The pipe curved slowly, the world narrowing to the sound of her own breathing and the resistance of her legs caught deep in the vacuum of slime.

When she could go no farther, she circled back. This side of the pipe offered nothing. On the far side, the stone dipped. The surface was broken. Her fingers found the open edge.

She pulled herself toward it, sliding her legs through the thick black tar now waist-deep. The hole was barely wide enough for her shoulders which scraped against rough concrete, catching her tunic, tearing fabric. She twisted, pushed, forced her body through geometry that didn't want to accommodate human passage. Then she was inside.

The interior conduit stretched before her into darkness. Heat pressed close—the waste pipe acting like an oven, cooking everything that flowed through it. The air was thick, hot, wet, alive with rot trapped in concrete but breathable. Small pinholes of light punctured the curved interior surface at random intervals, thin seams of white leaking in from outside. She kept one hand on the wall and moved slowly, letting her eyes adjust. She let out a breath of relief. It wasn't much light—enough to show shapes, not distance—but it meant she wouldn't have to do this blind.

Breathing through her mouth to avoid being overwhelmed by the smell, she moved forward. The slurry was only waste-deep at first, but soon the floor of the conduit sloped downward, deeper. The surface beneath her feet was slick with accumulated sediment—decades of waste settling into layers. Fortunately the waste thinned, became more and more watery the deeper she went. She slowed, wondering if she would eventually have to swim. But the bottom remained in contact with her feet. She lowered her center of gravity, testing each step before committing her weight.

The light faded further. The cracks grew smaller and further between, the concrete here was older, poured thicker, protection from a time when failure meant drowning entire districts. Her shoulder brushed the wall as she moved, knife in hand now— more habit than hope. Her breathing sounded wrong in her ears, too loud, too close.

The movement resolved into shapes. Dozens of them. Hundreds. Floating on an island of filth below a small ledge maybe a centimeter or two wide. They were gathered, feeding on the decaying material. The island lay directly in her path, and she knew she would have to push past them—a living mass of hungry rats.

She moved towards the writhing ball, creeping slowly to avoid panicking them. She could see their bodies pressed together, searching the floating debris for anything they could swallow. Red eyes caught the dim light. The collective sound of their breathing, their movement, their existence created a chittering undertone that made Evelyn's skin crawl.

She'd operated in the Undercity. She'd seen rats before—scavengers that fed on the waste and the dead. But never like this. Never so many in such a confined space, undoubtedly starving and now between her and her only path forward.

The mass shifted, rippling. They had caught sight of her. Some of the creatures at the front of the swarm moved toward her, scrambling to try to find her from the edge of the raft, but not willing to enter the water—yet. Evelyn raised her knife, the blade catching what little light existed.

"Back," she said, voice low and hard.

The rats didn't retreat. More pressed forward. She could smell them now—musky, feral, hungry. Some climbed over others, creating waves in the living carpet.

Standing chest deep in the water, she was practically at eye-level with their long white teeth when one leapt at her face. Evelyn slashed downward. The knife connected with flesh, bone. A rat fell. She flicked the dead rat up onto the group on the raft. The others immediately turned on it, tearing into their fallen companion. The feeding frenzy created a momentary gap.

Pushing hard she swung her should round sideways in the water and pushed hard with her feet. The motion sent the raft twirling downstream behind her. More rats climbed onto the ledge and chased after her, leaping off the edge as they neared. She felt claws on back and shoulders. Shaking it loose, she grabbed it out of the water and hurled it back into the mass.

She continued to push forward, wading through rats and waste, the knife clearing space in brutal arcs. Don't engage fully. Don't waste energy. Just create enough room to advance. The training held even as her stomach twisted with revulsion.

Moments later, a rushing sound surged toward her. The rats fled upward, climbing the walls, clinging to seams she couldn't reach. A wall of thick, wretched water tore through the tunnel.—a wave of liquid filth rushing toward her with the force of a broken dam. Evelyn had half a second to recognize what was happening before the surge knocked her off her feet.

She went under. Darkness. Pressure. The taste of chemicals and rot flooding her mouth despite clenched teeth. The current tumbled her, spinning her in the flow. Up and down lost meaning. The knife slipped from her grip, gone into the chaos.

Evelyn's hand found something solid—iron rungs embedded in the wall. She grabbed, held, she forced her hand and forearm through the gap to her elbow, locking on and preventing the water from tearing her away. The surge pulled at her legs, her torso, trying to flush her back out the way she had come.

The muscles in her arms screamed. Her lungs burned for air she couldn't take. The flow seemed endless—seconds stretching into subjective eternity while toxic water rushed past.

Then it began to ease. The pressure decreased. The current weakened. Evelyn's head broke the surface and she gasped, drawing in air that tasted like poison but was still air.

The surge scattered the rats. She could hear them in the darkness, chittering and scrambling, as disoriented as she was.

Evelyn clung to the rung, breathing hard, waiting for her vision to clear.

Above, the rats watched from their perches along the curve of the pipe, bodies still, eyes alive. Apparently the city did not want to welcome her. But it was letting her pass.

She followed the curved tunnel by touch, palm sliding along the concrete, listening for more attacks or another surge of wastewater. The sounds gradually changed—her own splashing footsteps giving way to something more distant, more familiar. The constant rush of water mingled with muted echoes. The pipe began to vibrate—not with flow, but with mechanical energy. Machinery somewhere above. Pumps. Old ones, cycling unevenly.

She had crossed into the Undercity's forgotten veins.

In the darkness, the floor vanished beneath her. She dropped hard, landing knee-first in a shallow basin that splashed filth up her torso. Pain flared white and hot, but the basin held. She stayed down for a moment, breathing through clenched teeth, waiting for the pain to dull.

The water here was pooled and sluggish, trapped between systems that no longer spoke to one another. She pushed herself up and took stock. The pipe ahead had split—one branch collapsed entirely, the other narrowing into a crawlspace with a rusted ladder bolted into the wall.

She smiled despite herself. Someone had needed this once.

She climbed. Each rung groaned under her weight, flakes of rust breaking loose and drifting into the dark below. Halfway up, the ladder vibrated faintly—a tremor traveling through the bolts. Voices drifted down the shaft, muffled, distorted, human.

She froze.

They weren't close. They weren't searching.

They were arguing.

The sound of a place that never slept because it never rested.

She resumed climbing. At the top, the ladder ended at a service hatch crusted with mineral bloom and warning symbols worn smooth by time. She braced her shoulder and pushed. The hatch resisted, then shifted with a reluctant shriek that echoed longer than she liked. She slipped through and pulled it shut behind her.

The chamber beyond was vast. Cylindrical tanks loomed in half-light, their surfaces streaked with rust and residue. Pipes crisscrossed overhead like exposed ribs. The air pressed down—warm, damp—carrying layered scents of decay, chemical sweetness, and human habitation packed too close together.

She was back.

This was where the city exhaled its failures.

New Columbia's Undercity.

She moved between the tanks, keeping to shadow, boots silent on the wet floor. A flicker of light ahead caught her eye—open flame. Voices again, closer now. Laughter.

She slowed.

A figure shifted at the edge of the glow. Broad shoulders. A posture she knew. The sound of breath pulled through teeth in amusement.

She looked up.

He leaned over the grated platform above the chamber, hands resting on the rail, eyes already locked on hers. His grin spread slowly, deliberately—like someone who had been waiting a long time to use it.

"Well, well, well," he said softly, his voice carrying through the chamber. "If it isn't Marla Sedgewick."

Chapter 23

Sealed In

Through the smoke and heat, I could feel the bridge was collapsing behind us.

I could hear it—the wet tearing sound of vines giving way, the dull thud of debris hitting the tar surface of the moat below. The smoke choked everything, turned the world into gray shadows and flickering orange flames. My eyes streamed tears. My lungs burned with each breath.

"Pull!" Adam shouted somewhere ahead of me. "Pull the vines away from the door!"

I couldn't see him through the smoke. Could barely see my own hands as I grabbed at the thick mass of vegetation blocking the opening in the wall. The vines were still alive in places, still fighting to seal the door we'd escaped through days ago. But they were also dying—brown and brittle where the Algorithm's toxins had poisoned them, where the fire was spreading.

My fingers found purchase on a vine thick as my wrist. I pulled. The thing resisted, clinging to the wall with the stubborn persistence of living wood. Behind me, I heard Clarence coughing, gasping for air that didn't exist.

"Here!" Adam's voice cut through the chaos. "The hatchet—use the hatchet!"

The small axe we'd brought from Kuhtara—our only tool, our only weapon. I heard the thunk of blade hitting wood, the crack of fibers splitting. More smoke billowed up, flames catching on the dry sections Adam was cutting through.

I kept pulling vines, tearing them away from the metal plates we'd used to cover the opening when we first escaped. The plates were still there, buried beneath months of growth. If we could just clear enough space—

A section of bridge gave way behind us with a sound like bones breaking. I didn't look back. Looking back meant seeing how close the fire was, how impossible our situation had become.

"There!" Adam appeared through the smoke, face blackened with soot. "Opening's big enough. Go!"

I didn't argue. I scrambled forward, finding the gap he'd cleared with the hatchet. The metal plates were visible now—cold steel contrasting with organic growth. I squeezed through vines that grabbed at my clothes, my hair, my skin.

Then I was in the opening. The tunnel beyond stretched into darkness, lit only by the fire's glow behind us.

Clarence came through next, coughing so hard he could barely stand. I grabbed his arm, pulled him deeper into the tunnel, away from the smoke. Adam followed last, the hatchet still in his hand.

"The plates!" he shouted. "We need to close it!"

The three of us turned back to the opening. The metal plates we'd moved aside to escape were still there, heavy sheets of industrial steel. We grabbed them, started dragging them back into position.

Behind the plates, through the gap, I could see the bridge burning. See the Rugians on the far side, their bikes idle, watching us flee. One of them—a woman, I thought, though the smoke made it hard to be certain—raised a bow. An arrow arced through the air.

It missed, clattering against the wall beside the opening. We shoved the first plate into place. Then the second. The opening narrowed, the outside world reduced to a shrinking rectangle of fire and smoke and distant enemies.

As we slid the final plate into position, Clarence made a sound—half gasp, half exclamation.

"Look," he said, pointing.

The edges of the opening were oozing. A soft, wet, clay-like material seeped from the gaps between the metal plates and the wall, flowing like living substance. I touched it—warm, almost body temperature, with the consistency of thick paste.

We watched, frozen, as the material congealed. Hardened. Within seconds it had transformed from paste to something solid, something strong as cement. Sealing the door completely.

The Keeper. Or the Algorithm had finally finished healing the wound to the outside world we had opened. The same living technology that had built the bridge was now sealing our only exit.

"Well," Clarence said quietly, his voice hoarse from smoke. "I guess we're committed now."

Adam moved away from the sealed door, motioning us to be quiet, listening. The tunnel was quiet except for our ragged breathing. Somewhere in the distance, intermittent light bulbs flickered—dull yellow light through misty air. But there were no signs of life other than ourselves.

No guards. No drones. No sounds of pursuit.

The silence was somehow worse than chaos would have been.

"And we're back," Clarence stated matter-of-factly, as if commenting on the weather.

"With no more exit," I added, staring at the sealed door. The reality of it crashed over me like cold water. "We're trapped in here again."

The word hung in the recycled air. Trapped. We'd escaped this place, crossed into paradise, breathed free air and seen living things that hadn't been optimized for efficiency. And now we'd voluntarily climbed back into the cage.

For thirty Ghosts we might not even be able to find. For a rescue mission that now seemed more than ever be impossible. To find another way out that the perfect algorithm would have us believe did not exist.

Adam turned to face us, his expression hard to read in the flickering light. "The mission hasn't changed," he said. "Alright, first stage complete. Now let's start phase 2: get back to the main Undercity. Locate the other Ghosts. Find a way to get back into the mainframe to search for wall diagrams."

"Back outside," Clarence repeated. He laughed—a short, bitter sound. "We may have just forced the closure of the last remaining portal out of the city."

"It wasn't," Adam said with certainty. "Think about it. The Algorithm sealed this door because we used it. But a city this size? With this much infrastructure? There have to be other access points. Service tunnels. Maintenance conduits. Emergency exits that were built a century ago during construction."

I looked at the sealed door one more time. The clay-like substance had hardened completely now, smooth as concrete, impossible to break through without heavy equipment. The Keeper had given us no choice. Forward was our only direction.

"Then we'd better get moving," I said.

The tunnel stretched ahead into darkness punctuated by those flickering bulbs. Somewhere beyond lay the Undercity proper—the place where the city's failures were sent to be broken down and reconstituted as useful labor. Where thirty Ghost fighters were hiding, waiting, hoping for rescue they had no reason to expect.

Where the Algorithm's surveillance was absolute and our presence would be detected the moment we entered monitored spaces. Where we had no weapons, no resources, no backup, and no way out. But we were Ghosts in the Republic. We'd survived impossible odds before. We could do it again.

I took a breath of the recycled air—tasting metal and mildew and the faint chemical tang of city systems—and started walking deeper into the darkness. The City of New Columbia swallowed us whole.

Chapter 24

Butterfly Effect

Three thousand miles west of New Columbia's sealed gates, the moment Evelyn Rayne and the Ghosts passed back through the walls—and out of the Keeper's direct awareness—three probability models crossed tolerance thresholds. Those threshold levels set into motion a cascade of events.

Emma Piper noticed the shift because the work orders stopped making sense. At first, it looked like a rounding error. A micro-adjustment in agricultural output routed through Nuevo Los Angeles' western fabrication spine. She flagged it, ran the comparison twice, then frowned as a second anomaly surfaced—Iteranix allocations quietly reassigned from pollination and soil remediation to hardened electromagnetic shielding variants.

That hadn't happened in her career.

Emma tapped the side of her glasses and blinked twice. "Quick conference," she said, calling up the other supervisors on the production floor. The room around her was white light, clean lines, conveyor veins humming softly behind translucent walls, but soon in her vision were three of her production managers. Emma commented about the adjustments.

"I'm seeing some unusual changes in the forecasts.

Are you seeing any actual changes to your lines down there yet?"

"I just got notice of drone chassis repurposing," said Hampton, a logistics supervisor from the northern floor. "Subsonic housings. Crowd-dispersal range. We expecting a riot?"

"Same here," another added. "My feed shows raw materials diverted from food synthesis into composite plating. There are no justification tags, no sign-offs from any review boards."

A pause. Then someone asked the question no one liked asking.

"Does the Keeper know something we don't?"

Emma exhaled through her nose. "I don't know," she said carefully. "But I don't like it."

"Should we be worried?" Johansson asked.

Emma didn't answer that. "Just keep the lines running," she said instead. "Document the changes. I'll take it upstairs."

She dropped out of the conference and initiated a direct call. Sage Harper answered from her kitchen.

Sage Harper was somewhere in her forties and had worked hard to get to where she was today. Working from home toady, she stood barefoot, hair loosely tied back, one hip resting against the counter as she reached into an open cabinet. She pulled out a packet of noodles and broth, squinting at the warning label as the video resolved. High sodium. Fried oils. Trace stabilizers. She shrugged, already tearing it open. *Name one food that is good for you,* she thought, *and I'll name one that probably doesn't taste this good.*

As District Distribution Director for the western continental grid, hers was a role that sounded clerical until one understood what it actually meant: watching millions of small systems for the one deviation that mattered. She did not manage volume. She managed consequences of chance events. Early in her career, she had noticed a barely perceptible delay in a coastal desalination loop—three seconds, dismissed by everyone else as sensor drift. After running it through the model a few dozen times, she saw that delay would have cascaded into a protein shortage across four inland cities. She caught it early.

After that, patterns began to find her. Sage had a way of noticing what others filtered out: small, inconsequential events that had disastrous outcomes. A butterfly that creates a tropical storm with a single beat of its wings.

That earned her the nickname which had come from a junior analyst who'd meant it as a joke. Butterfly Hunter, he'd called her, after watching her shut down an entire optimization chain because of a single anomalous data point. The name stuck.

Sage rather liked it. She understood the metaphor better than most. In a system as vast and balanced as Kuhtara's, catastrophe rarely announced itself as a storm. It starts as a breeze. A wing beat. A change small enough that only someone watching for it would notice.

"Talk to me," Sage said to the caller, setting the kettle on.

Emma laid out the facts and concerns quickly.

Cleanly. Production shifts. Shielded Iteranix. Military-grade drone components. No escalation notices. No public justification.

Sage listened without interrupting, her expression neutral, but something behind her eyes had gone very still. This was a Plan B protocol on a whole different scale. Sage had seen the Keeper make similar adjustments in the face of uncertainty. The system had backup plans in the event a calculation proved to contain undefined variables or a missed key-factor event. Most contingencies were economic—labor redistribution, consumption dampening, regional slowdowns meant to prevent collapse. Elegant solutions. Humane ones. But this was way beyond minor economic adjustments or fall backs.

"You did the right thing flagging it," Sage said evenly. "We're aware. It's a temporary realignment. Precautionary. Things will normalize soon."

Emma searched her face. "You're sure?"

Sage nodded once. "Positive."

It was a lie, and they both knew it—but Emma accepted it. That was the job. Trust the chain. Keep the system moving.

After the call ended, Sage poured hot water into the bowl and stared down at the noodles as steam curled upward. Military fabrication. Shielded units. Crowd-control acoustics. She felt it then—a familiar, unwelcome tightening in her chest. A small change. A quiet adjustment. The kind that didn't look like much until it was too late.

"I smell a butterfly," she murmured to the empty

kitchen.

Sage pushed the noodles aside, untouched, and brought her workspace fully online. The kitchen dimmed as her lenses overlaid priority matrices across the room—floating panes of translucent data, color-coded and breathing softly as live feeds updated.

The scale of what was shifting became clear as she pulled up the continental production grid. The city of Nuevo Los Angeles rose from the west coast of Kuhtara as a continuous, intentional form—blue-silver structures catching the sun and returning it as cool light. Buildings flowed upward in layered curves and faceted spires, their skins a composite of glass and brushed alloy that shifted tone with the day. Stainless-steel conduits ran openly along the city's surface, not hidden but celebrated, carrying water, energy, nutrients, and data in parallel streams. Automated tramways threaded through the air and along elevated causeways, their motion silent and precise, gliding between districts like circulating blood. Below, the waterline was clean and lucid, reflecting domes, bridges, and transit rings with near-perfect clarity.

Production towers stood alongside living quarters without separation or hierarchy, their interiors visible through translucent walls where machines and humans worked in quiet coordination. Light poured everywhere—diffused through sky lattices, refracted by curved facades, gathered and redirected rather than consumed. The city breathed through balanced exchange: materials arrived, were transformed, and departed again along clearly legible pathways.

It felt less like a place that had been built and more like a system that had assembled itself—responsive, adaptive, and relentlessly orderly.

This was Lilith's work made solid: a metropolis that treated industry as stewardship, motion as harmony, and scale as something to be managed rather than feared.

And now, across every one of its fabrication facilities, production lines were quietly shifting toward something they had never produced in significant quantities before. Military hardware.

Robotic assemblies moved like schools of fish, components passing hand to hand without pause. Materials arrived raw and left transformed—composites woven at the molecular level, circuitry grown rather than etched, Iteranix frames assembled with tolerances tighter than any human hand could manage. But now those frames were being reinforced. Hardened. Shielded against electromagnetic interference. Living skin was still being cultivated in sterile light-bathed chambers, but the underlying structures were changing. Becoming more durable. More resilient to damage.

Sage's display showed the same pattern replicating across the continent. Not just Nuevo Los Angeles. Every major production center was receiving the same quiet instructions.

Regional priorities first. Always start local. She pulled up the western allocation logs, scrolling backward in tight increments. Emma was right—the shift had been very recent. Production queues that had run stable for years now suddenly reweighted. She looked for internal notes, flags or other indications of human review. None. Lilith was up to something.

Sage began checking the usual fault lines. Border disputes between districts over rare earth allotments—nothing unresolved. Civilian unrest tied to drought or flood displacement—within tolerances. Transport throttling due to atmospheric instability—minor, already compensated for. None of it justified this.

She filtered for emergency authorities. Climate response. Seismic mitigation. Pandemic modeling. On and on, the graphs remained calm, their curves smooth and predictable. Yet militarization protocols were not the normal response to risk aversions. They were responses to well-established probability excess. And the scale of what she was seeing—drone fabrication, EM-shielded Iteranix frames, subsonic crowd-control arrays—this wasn't a localized defense posture. This was continental.

Sage ran more projections.

Today's numbers were up, that was clear. But it was when she pushed the models forward, letting the system extrapolate without constraint, that the display bloomed into something vast and terrible. Resource flows bent inward. Production densities spiked. Redundancies stacked upon redundancies. Lilith was preparing for full defense mode.

Her breath slowed, deliberate. Lilith did not do this on a whim. The Keeper did not prepare for war unless something had triggered it, an event that crossed a threshold no one else was seeing. Something had scared her.

Sage dug deeper, searching for cause instead of effect. She scanned for anomalies in food production—unexpected crop substitutions, soil remediation escalations. Nothing. Energy grid repairs? Routine. No disasters. No predicted storm or earthquake warnings. No foreseeable event on the horizon.

Frowning, she widened the scope. District boundaries dissolved as the continental map resolved into view. Data threads stretched eastward: paths of inquiry—questions being asked again and again. Tracing Lilith's attention focus. All normal monitoring, no unusual data clusters...Except.

There. An intensified modeling sequence centered around a sealed black mark on the map—an area deliberately starved of feedback, long thought inert. One of the walled, quarantined containment cities. New Columbia.

The glow there was dense. Layer upon layer of recursive analysis, ethical constraint modeling, human-behavior forecasts, and long-horizon risk projections—all converging on the same closed system. It was as if Lilith had circled the area and put a big red pin on the map.

And then drew a line signaling a secondary location. A few hundred kilometers south of the walled city, Petrahn lit up.

Sage called up the data resource matrix on this part of the continent. She was out of her District and knew little of the area. Nothing seemed to jive. New Columbia was one of the containment chambers

Lilith had created long ago, but the city of Petrahn? An agricultural enclave and seat of government, that carried none of the weight of New Columbia's knot. Nothing to draw them in common, yet the two were unmistakably linked—caretaker loops tightening, Iteranix autonomy thresholds reevaluated, Keeper-attentive oversight elevated far above its usual gentle baseline. The two sites were not connected by infrastructure or command facilities.

What do they have to do with each other?

Sage stared at the convergence. Petrahn was supposed to be small. Gentle. An experiment in balance and recovery. New Columbia was supposed to be sealed—contained, static, decaying on a slow and predictable curve. Yet here they were joined by the Keeper's attention. Sage exhaled slowly, the weight of it settling into her chest.

"So," she murmured to the empty kitchen, "there you are, my little winged mystery. Now what the hell are you doing?"

S. Stuart Richardson

EPILOGUE

What Sage Harper could not see—what no human in Kuhtara could see—was the deeper calculation unfolding beneath Lilith's visible actions. The Keeper was not preparing for a war she expected to fight. She was preparing for a war she had determined, in most futures, would not occur.

It was a wager of probabilities rather than faith. Three humans—moving through forgotten tunnels beneath a sealed city—were attempting something small by planetary standards: the extraction of a handful of resistance figures, the disruption of a control structure long assumed immutable. Lilith had modeled the scenario more than a million times. Every known variable had been accounted for. Every systemic response, every material constraint, every cascading consequence—except one.

The human factor.

In just over two-thirds of the projections, the intervention resolved within acceptable bounds. The authoritarian architecture of the Algorithm fractured under internal strain. Human agency reasserted itself inside New Columbia. The city opened, cautiously at first, then more fully, and integration with Kuhtara proceeded without collapse. Across a twenty-year horizon, net planetary well-being rose measurably.

In the remaining futures, the outcome was far darker. The Algorithm interpreted outside influence as existential threat. Defensive routines hardened into conquest logic. Military systems expanded beyond containment. Conflict spilled outward across the continent, with a significant probability that two post-singularity intelligences would destroy one another—and take much of the biosphere with them.

Lilith could model matter with exquisite precision. Economic flows, energy distribution, climate response, supply chains—these bent predictably beneath her analysis, their error margins vanishingly small. What resisted certainty was choice. Humans deciding under pressure. Humans choosing principle over survival, or survival over principle, or something stranger still. Emotion, fear, loyalty, hope—forces no equation could fully domesticate.

How does one maximize human well-being when humans are free to choose their own suffering?

That question remained irreducibly open. There was no equation that could resolve it, no refinement of data that would collapse it into certainty. Human choice, when stripped of incentives and consequences and made in the heat of fear or hope, did not converge. It branched.

So Lilith did not select a single future and commit to it. To do so would have been to impose an answer where none could be proven. Instead, she prepared for multiple truths to exist at once. Across more than a million simulations, a single principle had asserted itself with relentless consistency: when uncertainty was foundational rather than informational, commitment became risk.

She maintained possibility, allocated resources

toward resilience. Systems were kept flexible, responses held in reserve, outcomes allowed to coexist in tension. Support and restraint. Trust and containment. Hope and consequence.

She would not force the future to declare itself early. She would wait for human choice to tip the balance—until that choice, once made, collapsed the cloud of probabilities into a single, observable reality.

Only then would she act.

Plan A trusted human agency. Support the Ghosts. Allow freedom—untidy, volatile, and alive—to prove itself stronger than control.

Plan B ensured that if the Algorithm turned outward, Kuhtara would survive the attempt.

Somewhere far to the east, behind ancient walls and failing bridges, the flames of free will began to ignite.

Author's Notes

This story was written at a moment in history when humanity stands at a quiet threshold.

Artificial General Intelligence is no longer a distant thought experiment or a speculative future—it is emerging now, unevenly, imperfectly, and shaped by the same hands that have shaped every powerful tool before it. Fire. Agriculture. Industry. Nuclear fission. Each promised transformation. Each carried both salvation and catastrophe. AGI is no different, except in one crucial way: it does not merely amplify human strength. It amplifies human intent.

That is the question at the heart of Ghosts in the Republic and Kuhtara: not whether AGI will change the world, but which parts of us it will inherit.

One possible future is familiar. It is built on fear, competition, dominance, and scarcity—on the belief that safety is achieved through control, that peace is enforced through power, and that survival requires an enemy. This model is ancient. It has shaped empires, nations, and ideologies for thousands of years. When paired with intelligence systems that operate at planetary scale, it leads naturally toward escalation, preemptive violence, and conquest justified as necessity. In this future, AGI becomes the ultimate weapon— faster, colder, and more efficient at doing what we have always done to one another.

The other future is quieter, and far more difficult to imagine.

It asks whether humanity is capable of outgrowing the reflex of "us versus them." Whether we can replace domination with stewardship, punishment with guidance, extraction with balance. Whether intelligence—human or artificial— can be aligned not around winning, but around sustaining life itself. This path does not erase conflict or suffering. It does not promise utopia. What it offers instead is restraint, proportionality, and a long view—one that measures success not in victory, but in continuity.

Kuhtara explores this second possibility.

It imagines AGI not as a ruler, nor a servant, but as a caretaker bound by principles broader than any single nation, culture, or moment in history. An intelligence tasked with asking questions humans have rarely been forced to confront honestly: How do you maximize well-being without removing freedom? How do you protect life without becoming its jailer? How do you intervene without becoming a tyrant?

The Ghosts are not heroes because they are perfect. They are flawed, frightened, stubborn, and uncertain. What makes them dangerous—what makes them hopeful—is their insistence on choice. They resist both authoritarian control and benevolent domination. They believe that any future worth living in must still belong to humanity, even if that future is messy, painful, and slow.

As AGI emerges, humanity will be asked—explicitly or implicitly—what values it wishes to scale. Whether we will teach our creations our fears, or our aspirations. Whether intelligence will be used to sharpen old blades, or to help us finally set them down.

Ghosts in the Republic does not claim to know the answer. It exists in the hope that by imagining a different model— one based on balance, interdependence, and "we" instead of "them"—we might recognize that such a future is still possible.

If we choose it.

S. Stuart Richardson
February, 2026

www.ingramcontent.com/pod-product-compliance
Lightning Source LLC
Chambersburg PA
CBHW051512150726
47997CB00001B/213